# The Trouble with Seasons

A Nash Adams Mystery
Book 8

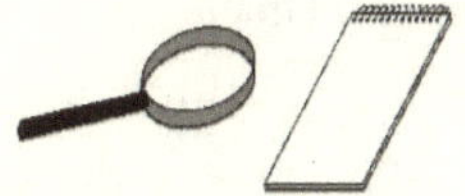

by

G. L. GRACIE

# Table of Contents

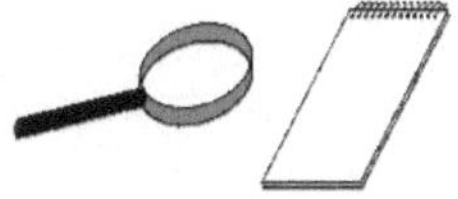

## 1

<hr>

The small oscillating fan worked in tandem with the struggling window air conditioner to battle the mid-July heat wave. It was a battle the machines were in danger of losing. Nash Adams, personal investigator, sat at his desk in his second-floor office above Meijer's deli. Drowsy from the intense heat, he leaned back in his chair tipping it on its rear legs and putting his feet comfortably up on his desk. His eyes drifted shut.

Young Anne Meijer sat at a second desk staring at the computer screen in front of her. Anne was the daughter of the proprietors of Meijer's Deli and Nash Adams' right-hand girl. The fourth day of the blistering heat wave had taken its toll on everyone. Anne's mind wandered—something that was not normal for the shy, dedicated young woman. However, even thoughts of a day at the lake did not take away the heat and lethargy affecting her body. She roused from her drowsiness to see a woman standing at the office door. She quickly sat up straight and leaned toward the sleeping Nash. It was unlike Anne to be caught off-guard.

"A-hem," she cleared her throat before whispering, "Nash, we have company."

Nash's feet hit the floor as he rubbed his eyes and tried to shake off his fatigue. Anne immediately stood and walked to the mini-fridge.

Nash focused on the woman who was posed with one hand raised against the door frame as if she were the center figure for a magazine layout. Her appearance seemed to suggest she had been standing there for some time.

"Hello," Nash managed to verbalize as he struggled to his feet. "I'm Nash Adams. How can I help you?"

"If you are indeed Nash Adams, then I suspect you're the person I came to see," the woman smiled.

She was strikingly beautiful with streaks of white in her dark hair that appeared to be more of a fashion statement than age-related. Her eyes were blue—not the soft blue of a summer sky, but the dark blue of an impending storm. They commanded his attention. She wore white slacks with an over blouse of filmy chiffon. Its navy color was interrupted only by splotches of blue and white flowers that seemed to match the vivid color of her eyes. The fabric was loose with flutter sleeves that gave the appearance of both comfort and freedom. She wore silver hoop earrings and an assortment of silver bracelets adorned her right arm. Her left arm was bare, but there were several silver rings on her left hand. Her makeup was meticulously in place as if the woman stood in a winter's breeze while Nash and Anne wiped perspiration from their faces.

"Come right on in," Nash greeted her. "And have a seat."

Efficient Anne was already handing their guest a bottle of cold water, which she graciously took. In one graceful movement, the woman appeared to float into the chair across the desk from Nash. She crossed her shapely legs that flowed down into a pair of white and navy sandals.

"So, how can I help you?" Nash reiterated as he placed a pad of paper and pencil in front of him and tried desperately to look professional while ignoring the heat and a pesky fly that had been awakened by the intrusion.

"I'd like to hire you, Mr. Adams. That is, if you are interested and available."

"Well, let's hear what's on your mind," Nash began, "uh, Ms,—uh—I didn't catch your name."

"It's Season—Mrs. Holiday Season," she said, with a smile that challenged the disbelief they could not hide.

Anne's jaw dropped for a second, but she quickly recovered while Nash forced his eyes to the notepad where he carefully wrote out the name.

"I realize it's somewhat of an unusual name, Mr. Adams. Let me explain. My father was a huge fan of the old west, specifically, a legend by the name of Doc Holliday. He was, of course, unaware that the man I married would give my name a whole new meaning. People usually just call me Holly."

"I hope you aren't going to ask me to become your deputy and ride a horse," Nash replied with a half-grin. "And, please, call me Nash. Mr. Adams sounds too formal."

Anne rolled her eyes at her boss. Holly pretended to ignore his poor attempt at humor.

"Mr. Season, bless his soul, and I had four daughters. They are grown now. They are all quite beautiful. I have a rather large house, so they all live at home with me. Anyway, I fear one of them has seen fit to remove a series of antiques from the house, and although they are entitled to everything I have once I've gone, this, to me, is robbery. I would like for you to see if you can find out which one of my darlings would dare do such a thing. I expect you to be discreet, however. I do not wish to accuse anyone of anything until I'm sure of what I'm dealing with."

"Won't they be suspicious if I contact them?"

"No. They already know I am aware of the missing pieces. I warned them that I was seeking professional help concerning their disappearance. I just want your opinion after you've interviewed them. I want to know which one is lying."

"Why not simply ask them?"

"At this point, I believe the trained eye of a professional is the best approach. I want to know which one is guilty, but

I don't want them to think I mistrust those who are innocent."

"When did you first notice the items were missing?" Nash asked pausing his own writing as Anne wrote furiously on her pad of paper.

"I know they were taken the night of July 10th."

"You seem sure of that."

"Yes, I know it was July 10th because my attorney and I had seen the items in question that evening. He thought it was time to re-evaluate them for insurance purposes. I can assure you they were all in place when I retrieved them, and I replaced them when we were through. He left at about 8:00 in the evening. I had a terrific headache, so I immediately took a hot bath and was in bed by 9:30 or so.

"My cook found the items missing the following morning when she came to work about 6 a.m. One of the doors to the display cabinet had been left open and drew her attention to it. I made a list of the missing items right afterward."

Holly rummaged through her bag and produced a list that she slid across the desk to Nash.

"Well, I believe we can help you with your situation," Nash agreed after briefly perusing the list.

"Excellent! I anticipated your answer and have set up a family dinner for Friday evening. I would like that to be your introduction to the family. But beware, Mr. Adams, my daughters are as smart as they are beautiful. You will find that you have your hands full."

"Understood," he murmured. Nash was uneasy that she had assumed he would take the case and had already set up a dinner for him to meet the girls, but he quickly recovered. This case clearly could have its issues if Mrs. Season was trying to run it.

They finished discussing the details of Nash's visit before she left. During their conversation, Nash had discovered Holly was a very wealthy client and wanted no expense spared. Nash remained gazing at the closed door, pondering the situation after she exited through it.

"All right!" Anne spoke up once they heard Holly's footsteps travel down the stairway and the bell on the deli door confirming she had left the building. "Who is Doc Holliday?"

Nash smiled. For all the knowledge she had crammed in her head, there were some things he was surprised his mild-mannered assistant still did not know.

"He was a dentist, a gambler, and a gunfighter from the early West, who was a friend to Wyatt Earp and his brothers." Nash explained. "Several of the Earp boys were lawmen. Most famous is perhaps the big fight between them and the Clanton Gang at the O.K. Corral. Doc Holliday, being a friend of the Earp brothers, joined in the fracas. He was in ill health with tuberculosis and died fairly young. He was a pretty colorful character."

"And you know all of this how?" Anne frowned.

"Guess I've read a few things about the old West in my time," Nash admitted. "That period in our history fascinates me."

Anne still seemed to have something bothering her.

"So, what did you think of Holly?"

"I think it would be very difficult being one of her daughters."

"Yeah. I wonder how poor Mr. Season died."

Anne remained quiet. Nash's experience had taught him that his assistant had something else on her mind.

"What is it? What are you thinking?" he finally asked.

"Really, Nash?" Anne frowned. "Holiday Season?"

2

←――――――――――――――→

Despite the stifling temperatures, Nash arrived at the project site by late afternoon on Thursday. The "project" began as an idea between Nash and his childhood-friend-turned-policeman, Louie. They had both run cross country in high school and had become close then. They still made time to run one or two times each week, and Louie was a frequent guest at the Adams' Sunday family dinners. After reminiscing about the changes the neighborhood had undergone since they were kids, they came upon a way to make a difference. Now, their initial idea was blossoming into reality, but it had been a long road for the aspiring personal investigator and the local detective.

With local businesses either closing or moving out of the area in recent years, their old neighborhood had deteriorated. The idea had been to find and restore a piece of real estate where kids and parents could once again bring their families together. The piece of land they had chosen was where their old elementary school had once stood. It was centrally located in the old neighborhood. It incorporated an entire city block so there was plenty of room for a variety of activities.

The old schoolhouse itself had deteriorated and most of it had been torn down. Only a remnant of the foundation remained. Trees and undergrowth had reclaimed the property. It had been years since the sound of children had been heard on the school playground.

Finding the property turned out to be the easy part. The less exciting time where they needed to prepare petitions and legal papers came next, followed by additional hours before the city council to convince them of the project's value. Finally, the city granted them the needed permission. Then they moved on to countless hours of soliciting funds. Nash was thankful his sister, Midge, and her boyfriend, Clark, gladly put in the time to make that happen.

Mr. Jackson, who owned a heavy equipment business in the neighborhood, donated his time to level out the remains of the school foundation. Although some of the land had been cleared, yard work was an ongoing constant process. Excited to see something happening in the area, slowly residents had arrived with rakes and wheelbarrows and push mowers when they noticed Nash and Louie working on the property. The task of removing or trimming bushes and trees came first, but then Mrs. Laughton asked if she could plant flowers—something that Ma Adams heartily endorsed.

Tony Adams, Nash's younger brother, had insisted that a makeshift basketball court and some swings for younger children be one of the first items to be erected. It proved to be a good idea. Once the word spread, children flocked to the new playground. Little by little, more people from the neighborhood wandered by, mostly out of curiosity. A vegetable garden was suggested for those who needed fresh produce in the summer. Nash saw that as a positive sign. Soon all those interested in helping were helping. Nash was a firm believer that being involved gave the neighbors a sense of ownership. Building materials were donated or purchased, and now a building for indoor activities was growing toward the sky.

The whole project had become a gathering place even before it was finished. However, it also attracted the attention of a few less-upright members of the neighborhood. Chief among them was a young man who had a leadership role in one of the local gangs. Both Nash and Louie knew of Spike's influence because it had sadly led to an increase in petty crime and graffiti. In some respects, their project had become Spike's personal project as well with him frequently stopping by to harass and threaten others. Thankfully, Spike's gang was content to use talk and not actions. Ma called them troublemakers. Louie could confirm her assessment since he recognized at least two or three of them from their previous run-ins with the law.

Today was no different than any other. As Nash and Louie started organizing the needed building materials for the evening's work, they heard the roar of Spike's Dodge Charger.

"Here they come," Louie whispered to Nash as three young men emerged from the sporty red car.

"Seems like they'd give up sooner or later," Nash sighed.

"I think it's funny how they keep coming back. I really think they're interested in what's going on."

"I think Spike's mostly blow. That's how he gets his power—by tearing down others. Still, I think he can be handled."

Spike was a young and arrogant high school drop-out. The scar he wore proudly across his forehead attested to the fact that he had been in several significant fights. It was doubtful that he had ever held a real job, but it had taken him several years of careful plotting and bullying to gain his reputation. His body-building routine had enhanced his short, stocky stature, but it was his dominant personality and his ability to intimidate that moved him to the position of gang leader.

Nash and Louie continued working, ignoring the three as they approached. Then, the young men just stood there watching, occasionally making snide remarks about the project. If their intent was to intimidate, it was not working. When they thought they were seemingly being ignored or viewed as merely one of the on-lookers Spike felt it necessary to make himself known. He decided to draw Nash and Louie's attention away from their work.

"So, I guess you're gonna keep on bein' do-gooders," he challenged, hoping to rankle Nash or Louie.

"Yes, we plan to keep moving forward," Nash agreed but kept on working without giving Spike the satisfaction of stopping their progress.

"You know, somethin' could happen to tear all this down. Maybe an earthquake or big wind or somethin' like that could come along." He glanced at his minions pointedly, and they obliged him by laughing.

"Yeah, that could happen, Spike," one of his pals said to encourage him.

"Maybe a fire—or some other unforeseen tragedy perpetrated by some angry citizen who resents you all and your dumb project." Spike continued, swelling with pride at his own comments that he truly believed were clever.

"You know this neighborhood pretty well, Spike." Nash remained calm and gave a soft answer. "I imagine you'd be able to tell us just who would be mean enough to do that."

Spike frowned. This was clearly not going as he had planned.

"We don't want nothin' like this goin' on in the neighborhood, understand?" Spike raised his voice with irritation. "This is our territory."

Once again, he looked to his buddies for approval while Nash was slow to answer.

"A neighborhood isn't just for a few people, you know. These kids and families have the right to have a place to go."

"How about my rights—me and my associates here?"

Grunts from the other two showed their agreement.

"Everybody has rights—as long as what you are doing is within the law," Nash countered.

"Yeah, I see you got a local cop supporting you," Spike acknowledged Louie's presence.

"I believe we've met before—on several occasions," Louie responded calmly.

Again, it was not the response Spike was hoping for. Nash went to retrieve a large piece of OSB stacked behind the gang members.

"Grab that end," he casually said to Spike who was immediately taken off-guard.

"What? You want me to help you?" Spike was indignant.

"Just thought you were probably the strongest guy around," Nash replied as he looked Spike square in the face for the first time since his arrival. "Of course, if you think it's too much for you or you can't handle it..."

Nash let the challenge penetrate Spike's brain.

Spike's eyes shifted uneasily. He did not wish to lose face with his buddies by helping, but at the same time, he could not ignore the insult to his physical strength if he refused to help. He reached down to pick up the OSB, insisting he could handle it entirely by himself. Nash yielded to Spike's decision, concealing the smile on his face. Louie, however, openly exhibited a broad smile.

Not willing to be labeled as a weakling, Spike continued to exhibit his strength by lifting other pieces of OSB and holding them in place so Nash could nail them. Sweat broke out on his forehead from the exertion, but he refused to stop. Before long, his two companions joined in as well while Nash and Louie exchanged knowing glances.

While the men had been working, Ma Adams arrived.

"Time for a break," Ma interrupted after a time. "I brought sandwiches and cookies and lemonade."

She offered them first to Spike and his friends, who readily helped themselves. Then, quite suddenly, as if they were embarrassed to be socializing with the do-gooders, Spike and his buddies made a quick exit.

"You think they'll be back?" Midge asked her brother.

"I'd bet on it," Nash responded.

Nash and Louie stayed after everyone else left, each quietly reflecting on the day's work and dreaming about the finished product.

"We need to name this place," Louie said. "We can't just keep referring to it as the 'neighborhood project.'"

"I've been thinking along those lines as well," Nash agreed.

"We had some good times here in elementary school."

"We sure did."

"Did a lot of growing up."

"Yep."

"And had a lot of good teachers—teachers who cared."

Nash heard the nostalgia in Louie's voice.

"I think I know exactly which teacher you're talking about," he said softly.

"I bet you do."

Louie turned to Nash with all the sincerity in his face.

"Do you think we could somehow dedicate this endeavor to her?"

"I was thinking the same thing. Somehow it seems fitting. Miss Ella Mae Swift! She sure made a big difference in a lot of kids' lives."

"Especially mine," Louie said with a thickness in his voice.

Louie had been in Miss Swift's fifth grade class when his mother took sick and died. It was Miss Swift who helped the young boy through some of the worst days of his life. Somehow, she always knew when Louie would need some lunch money or maybe a new pair of shoes. She did it humbly so Louie would not be embarrassed by the help. She often let him stay after school to help do whatever needed doing in the classroom just so he could spend some extra time with her and not have to go back to the lonely house that he shared with his father, who had drowned his sorrows in his own police work.

Although Louie received special treatment at the hands of Miss Swift, he was not the only one. There probably was not a former student alive who did not benefit from her care. She always seemed to know just what to say to make things better. She read extensively to her students from a wide variety of material and helped apply it to their daily lives. She knew how to make history come alive. She often sang or played music during school. She was even known to hit a few soft balls at recess or twirl the rope for the girls to skip. She was patient and kind, but demanding. She expected; therefore, she received. When the school day was finished, Miss Swift had taught a great deal more than math or science or language arts.

After making several attempts at just the right name, they settled on *Ella's Place: Ella's Place* it would be.

# 3

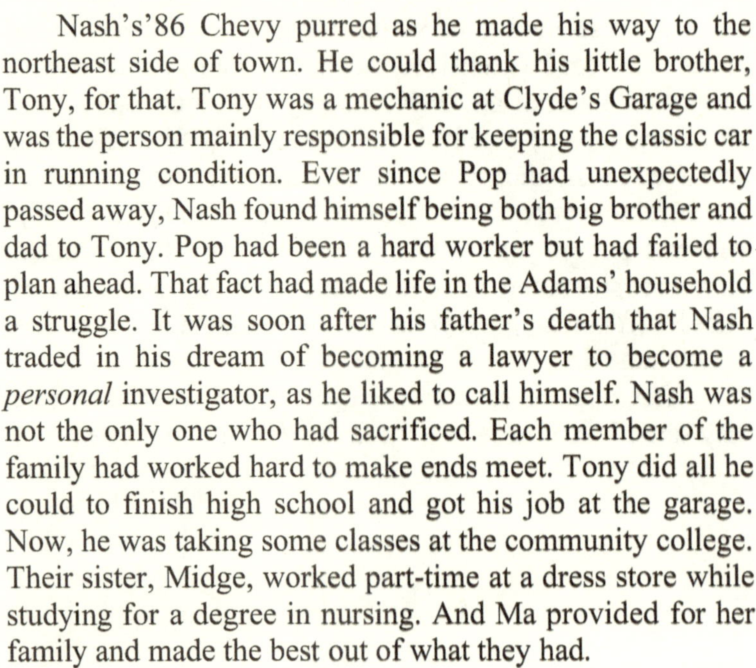

Nash's '86 Chevy purred as he made his way to the northeast side of town. He could thank his little brother, Tony, for that. Tony was a mechanic at Clyde's Garage and was the person mainly responsible for keeping the classic car in running condition. Ever since Pop had unexpectedly passed away, Nash found himself being both big brother and dad to Tony. Pop had been a hard worker but had failed to plan ahead. That fact had made life in the Adams' household a struggle. It was soon after his father's death that Nash traded in his dream of becoming a lawyer to become a *personal* investigator, as he liked to call himself. Nash was not the only one who had sacrificed. Each member of the family had worked hard to make ends meet. Tony did all he could to finish high school and got his job at the garage. Now, he was taking some classes at the community college. Their sister, Midge, worked part-time at a dress store while studying for a degree in nursing. And Ma provided for her family and made the best out of what they had.

Since there was no air conditioning in the car, breeze from the open window tousled Nash's light brown hair. He turned up the volume on the radio to listen to Garth Brooks' "We Belong to Each Other." Listening to the words brought thoughts of Katie to his mind.

Nash had met Katie on his first big case. He had asked her out on a whim to get more information about her employers, but she turned out to be someone he admired and respected. Even after he told her the truth about his initial motives, she stuck with him and became his girlfriend. She was smart and funny, and he loved spending time with her. As Nash sped along on his way to attend the Season family dinner, his heart was filled with pride for those he loved.

He found himself looking forward to dinner. Although it had been a busy Friday, he had grabbed a bit to eat earlier, but now his stomach was insisting that had not been sufficient.

Slowly, he emerged from the hubbub of city traffic into a more rural setting. His journey had taken him into an affluent area northeast of the city limits. Houses were far more spacious and somewhat secluded by acreage. Nash was not familiar with this area. His family lived in an old neighborhood where small family businesses struggled to survive and from which those who could afford it had long since moved to newer parts of town. Nash liked to refer to the houses in his neighborhood as "vintage."

He slowed the Chevy to concentrate on house numbers. He was glad the mailboxes were clearly marked because the houses themselves had become more concealed the farther from the city he traveled. After glancing again at the directions Holly had given him to confirm he had arrived at the correct place, he cautiously turned to drive through open iron gates onto a long, paved, tree-lined driveway. No house was yet visible.

Nash slowed the Chevy to a crawl as he viewed the wildness of his surroundings. Tall trees on either side of the driveway gave him the feeling of driving through a tunnel. As the car continued to negotiate the curving lane, he wondered if anything could be so far off the main thoroughfare. He contemplated the possibility that he must have made an error in calculating the route and began looking for a place to turn around on the narrow road when he saw the top of the mansion highlighted against the summer sky. He was awestruck as more of the entire picture came into view. In his line of business, he had encountered all kinds of homes, some of which were fabulous. This surpassed them all.

The imposing house towered above a huge fountain spewing sprays of water that glistened like silver in the sunlight. A massive flower garden, ablaze with vibrant color, encircled the fountain.

Strategically placed small shrubs nestled on the south side of the house while tall oaks sheltered its north. Someone had a good eye for design. The driveway made a wide turn in front of the house entrance before it circled around the flower garden and fountain on its way back to the main road. Situated at the front of the garden and rising above the flowers was an intricately lettered sign displaying the owner's last name: SEASON. Nash needed no other confirmation that he had reached his destination.

No sooner had Nash pulled to a halt in front of the main doors to the house than a man in full dress suit appeared. Nash recognized the expression on the man's face. He had seen that look before. He was sure the first words out of the man's mouth would tell him to either park his car in back where deliveries were made or remove it from the premises entirely. Surprisingly, the man opened the car door without a word, allowing Nash's lanky body to uncurl itself from the driver's seat, grabbing his sport coat as he went. He quickly buttoned his shirt collar and adjusted his tie before following the man to the house.

A welcome rush of cool air engulfed Nash's body as he stepped inside the foyer. He absently smoothed back his light brown hair, suddenly conscious that it might be out of place from the open car windows. Holly Season floated in from one of the other rooms to greet him.

"Thank you, Giles," she said as she dismissed the butler. "I will see to our guest."

"Very good, madam," Giles said and stiffly walked from the foyer.

"So glad you could make it, Mr. Adams—I mean, Nash," Holly said as she grasped his hand. "Welcome to the Season household."

"Thank you," Nash tried to be discreet as he looked around at the fabulous furnishings. He was immediately uncomfortable surrounded by such luxury. Paintings. Urns. Vases. Candelabra. Mirrors. Imported tile on the floor. Sculptured ceilings. The afternoon sun shining through the windows on either side of the entrance doors seemed to dance across every bit of glass and gold.

No less glamorous was Holly Season. Her hair, which earlier had been loose on her shoulders, was now pulled back in a more formal style. Her outfit, in that same beguiling color of her eyes, draped from her shoulders loosely, cinched at her slim waist, and culminated in wide-legged pants. Her delicate feet wore a series of straps pretending to be shoes.

"We can sit in this room," she gestured to a rather spacious room off to the right of the main entrance. "Dinner will be ready soon."

It was a pleasant room, less formal than the entryway. Live plants soaked up the sunshine from its many windows. Large bouquets of fresh flowers adorned every table in the room. A rather large stone fireplace occupied the inside wall. Above it was a portrait of a good-looking man who Nash assumed was Mr. Season.

Nash walked to the fireplace to get a better look at the portrait. Underneath it was a name etched in gold: Frederick "Stormy" Season. He controlled the urge to laugh. Stormy Season? He found it both amusing and strange.

As Nash settled into a wing-back chair, he was relieved to discover this furniture was more for comfort than appearance. He started to relax in his new surroundings.

"It was so good of you to come," Holly began as she reclined on a chaise lounge. "I believe the dinner atmosphere will be the perfect way to introduce you to my daughters. I hope it meets with your approval, but I have taken the liberty to set up visits with each of them individually next week. I have the dates and times written out for you on this piece of paper."

She reached out expectantly, and Nash rose to take the paper from her. Slightly bristling about having been told how to proceed with his investigation, he only glanced at the schedule she gave him before tucking it into the pocket of his sport coat. He refrained from speaking but decided to plan his next move based on how things played out this evening. Just then, a tinkling bell sounded from a room directly across the foyer.

"I believe that is our summons to dinner," Holly said with a smile as she rose to her feet.

Holly wove her arm through Nash's and headed with him to the dining room. He fully expected Giles to make a formal announcement of their arrival when they entered. It did not happen.

"I will sit at the far end of the table," Holly stated, and then waited for him to guide her there. Once seated she continued to direct him, "You will take the chair on the far end. The girls will sit on either side of the table—they already know their proper places. Brace yourself, Nash. You are about to enter an entirely different world."

Nash thought he already had entered that world.

Momentarily, three strikingly beautiful young women entered the room and took their places at the table. Although Nash remembered his manners and stood upon their entrance, none of them seemed to be either surprised or impressed with his presence. Each of them nodded toward him and remained silent as they slipped into their designated chairs. Giles and a rather frumpy short woman, who Nash guessed was the cook by her large chef's hat and apron, stood near the sideboard ready to serve the meal.

"Now, where *is* Summer?" Holly asked, clearly annoyed at the tardiness of one of her daughters.

No one else seemed to know or care.

Nash was beginning to contemplate what the consequences might be for showing up late for one of Holly Season's dinners, when he felt the rush of a body behind him. A young woman slid into the seat just to his left. Instead of responding to her mother's piercing look, she merely unfolded her napkin and clasped her hands together as if she were praying.

"Well—now that I see we are all here," Holly said with a scowl, "dinner may be served."

With that announcement, Giles and the cook snapped into action and began to uncover dishes and serve the food. The first course was shrimp cocktail.

"Girls, this is Mr. Adams—Nash," Holly began with a smile. "Nash, these are my four daughters. The one to your left who has finally decided to grace us with her presence, is my youngest, Summer."

Nash nodded to the attractive slender woman with short, curly blonde hair and a deep tan. She, in turn, smiled and winked her brown eyes at him flirtatiously as she slurped the sauce off her dipped shrimp in a most unladylike manner. He was quite sure he heard an exasperated sigh escape from Holly's lips.

"Seated next to Summer is my daughter, Spring. Spring is a nurse at Central Hospital. So far, all of her patients have survived."

*Ouch,* Nash thought, uncertain if Holly was trying to make a joke or being sarcastic.

Ignoring her mother's gibe, Spring briefly lowered her sunglasses to get a clearer view of the young investigator, revealing large, light blue eyes. "Thank you for joining us, Mr. Adams," she said with a quick bob of her head that made her shoulder-length, light brown hair bounce.

"This is Autumn," Holly continued as she gestured to the other side of the table. "She is our resident artist who someday will become famous and make our family proud."

Autumn raised a hand to acknowledge Nash's presence, then used it to lock some of her auburn hair behind her ear. After daintily dipping the shrimp in the cocktail sauce, she quickly allowed her deep brown eyes to meet his, but then they returned to her food as a faint blush traveled across her cheeks.

"And my eldest is seated to your right, Nash. This is Winter."

Winter leaned forward in her seat and locked her vivid blue eyes with his. "And at the head of the table is the one and only mother superior of the family, Mrs. Holiday Season, happily controlling all the details of our lives," she whispered with sarcasm equal to that of her mother. Just as her words were crisp and pointed, her chestnut hair was wrapped in a neat, tight bun.

The atmosphere around the Season dinner table was in stark contrast to the homey, uplifting feeling that permeated meals served in the Adams' household.

"Tell us about your family, Mr. Adams," Winter asked quickly before her mother could make any more comments.

Nash uncomfortably cleared his throat, wondering who was really being investigated.

"I am the oldest of three children. We all live with my mother. Our father passed away a few years ago. I have a younger sister, Midge, who is studying to be a nurse, like you, Spring." He shot Spring a smile. "My younger brother, Tony, works as a mechanic. I have been a personal investigator for about five years."

He paused a bit, but Winter kept looking at him expectedly with those stormy blue eyes that looked so much like her mother's while Giles and the cook cleared the now shrimpless cocktail glasses and exchanged them for bowls of French onion soup.

"I obviously can't talk about any of my cases for confidentiality reasons, but I have a neighborhood project I'm working on where we are creating a park and community building for children and families—a place where everyone can relax and enjoy life." Nash talked through the rest of the soup course and the entire salad course about the things Louie and he hoped to accomplish with their project. Only once the salad dishes were cleared away and the rack of lamb set before him did he begin to think he had rambled on about himself for too long.

"Tell me, Holly, how did you meet Mr. Season?" he asked, hoping to steer the conversation in a new direction. However, unlike his long diatribe, he soon discovered that communication was lacking in the Season household. Perhaps it was just the awkwardness of the introductions or perhaps this case would not be as simple as it was presented. Whatever the cause, he was finding it difficult to read each one of the girls.

They were well-into the main course when Nash felt something against his left leg. His first thought was that perhaps there was a dog in the house although he had not seen any signs of that. A wave of anxiety swept over him as the movement he felt traveled up and down his lower leg and he contemplated a second option. He stopped chewing and waited. His suspicions were right. Summer's bare foot was rubbing against him. Without calling attention to it, he discreetly moved his leg father away from her, hoping Winter would not get the same idea. As he did so, he heard a slight giggle coming from the chair to his left. He did everything he could to mask his response and to hide the flush of color that invaded his face.

Holly continued to dominate the conversation with tales of a trip to the Caribbean on Mr. Season's yacht for their honeymoon, while Nash watched for reactions from the four daughters. Summer was focused more on him than what her mother was saying, much to his chagrin. Autumn occasionally blushed when her mother mentioned some extravagance but otherwise remained focused on her food. The other two kept looks of mild disinterest plastered on their faces. Clearly, each daughter was clever at disguising her feelings.

When Holly finished her story, Nash tried to bring each of the girls into the conversation, but each question he directly asked them was answered by Holly. He soon realized conversation between family members was uncomfortable at best. Nash was relieved when Giles removed the main course dishes and served dessert. He had just taken one bite of the cherries jubilee when he saw Holly suddenly push back from the table. She first gagged and then began babbling about something foreign being in the room and making strange movements. The girls had clearly not been paying attention to what their mother was saying, so Nash was the first to notice.

"Holly, are you all right?" he asked from the far end of the table as he got to his feet.

Nash's abrupt movement, pulled Spring out of her inattention. She leaped to her feet to assist her mother.

"Giles, call 9-1-1," she shouted.

As Nash came around the table to assist, Winter had her cell phone out and was also calling for help. Summer and Autumn watched in horror. Although Giles was on his phone, the cook wailed and wrung her hands, causing the butler to move into the foyer to complete his call.

Minutes later sirens could be heard in the distant night air and soon the first responders arrived. Spring gave them a thumbnail version of the symptoms she had observed. Nash was pretty sure he heard the word "hallucinations." After their examination, the EMTs said they suspected that Holly Season may have had a reaction to some bad food, which sent the cook into another tizzy bemoaning that anything prepared in her kitchen might have caused such a thing.

"You mean we're all gonna die from something we ate?" Summer whined.

"Of course not, silly," Winter was impatient. "Try to remain calm. We don't know anything, yet, and no one else is sick."

"I think I might be," Summer said dramatically grasping her stomach and rolling her eyes back in her head.

"Get her out of here," Winter snapped, taking charge in her mother's place. Autumn, who had been consoling the cook, quickly took her and Summer to the sitting room.

Nash tried to take note of everything that was happening at once and was relieved when he heard Louie's friendly voice at the door. Louie and Nash frequently collaborated on cases.

"Good to see you," Nash said as he greeted Louie.

"What are you doing here?"

"Mrs. Season hired me and now—well, it's become a bit unusual and interesting."

Giving Nash a puzzled look, Louie set about the task at hand.

"What have we got here?" Louie asked the EMTs.

"Looks like some sort of poisoning. We're taking her in to check it out."

"I'll be here for a while," Louie said. "Let me know what you find out."

Louie proceeded to talk with Winter and Spring while Nash observed. Giles began to clear dishes from the table in the background until Louie told him that everything needed to remain as it was and then pulled him aside to question him. Once Autumn had successfully calmed Summer and the cook, Louie moved to question each of them as they reentered the dining room.

One observation Nash made during the interrogations was that none of the daughters seemed overly concerned for their mother. Even Summer had been more worried about being poisoned herself than her mother's health. He found that fact a bit strange, but it was only one of many questions that had surfaced in Nash's mind throughout the evening.

Louie had all but finished his interviews, including one that Nash overheard with the female servant that confirmed she was the Season's cook, Mrs. Snook, when Louie's cell phone rang.

"Yes? Yes. Really? Thanks for the information."

Louie gave a quick scowl in Nash's direction after he turned back toward the group.

"It appears," he announced, "the initial test results indicated that a poison was involved. Until we get specific details, I am declaring this an official crime scene. I will need all of you to remain in town and available for questioning."

The girls looked at each other in amazement while Mrs. Snook again burst into tears.

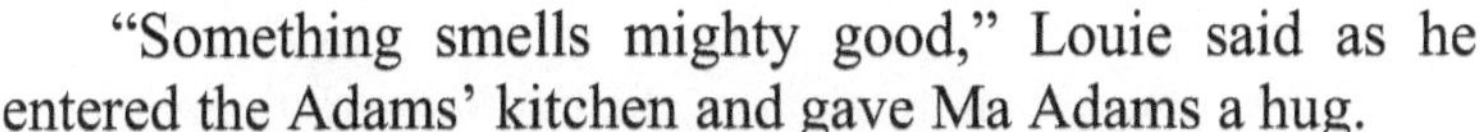

## 4

"Something smells mighty good," Louie said as he entered the Adams' kitchen and gave Ma Adams a hug.

"You always say that—every Sunday," Ma gently replied with a smile as she tied an apron over her Sunday church dress.

"And every word of it is true," Louie said as he took a sneak peek at the chocolate cake and cherry pie slices.

"Here, make yourself useful and carry this bowl of chicken and noodles to the table," Ma said as she pushed a rather large tureen into his hands.

"Comin' through," he announced when he met Katie on her way into the kitchen. "Hot food here."

"What can I do?" Katie asked Ma.

"There's mashed potatoes and green beans to dish up. And sliced tomatoes and a lemon gelatin salad in the fridge. Midge is setting the table. Tell her to be sure to put out Grandma Adams' salt and peppers."

"Sorry, I'm late," Anne announced as she came through the door. "There was a lot to do in the deli this morning."

"No problem," Midge assured her from the dining room. "You're just in time."

The Adams' family and friends gathered around the bountiful table for grace before they enjoyed the fruits of Ma's cooking. Stimulating conversation created a relaxed atmosphere—nothing at all like what Nash had experienced on Friday evening at the Season house. Whatever stresses the week might have dealt, one could be assured there would be refuge and comfort at that Sunday dinner table. Whereas the Season family table was dominated by monologues led by Holly, conversation at the Adams' table grew while the dinner guests satisfied their appetites.

"Nash, how did your dinner at the Seasons go?" Anne asked since she had not seen Nash since he left the office on Friday. "It probably didn't compare to this one."

"Well, it was very interesting to say the least." Nash replied, amazed that the shy, little, Jewish girl had grown brave enough to begin a conversation.

"Yes, very," Louie added as he exchanged glances with Nash.

"What does that mean?" Anne frowned, sensing something between the two men. "What are you not telling us? And, Louie, how do you know about the new client?"

"I was there also—at the Season home, Friday—later in the evening. I wasn't invited there for dinner though. Granted, I'm glad I wasn't," Louie chuckled, winking at Nash.

"What does that mean?" Midge's curiosity was aroused. "You guys are being way too secretive."

"Well, it seems the case became a little more complicated as the evening progressed."

"Tell us more," Midge prodded. Nash sighed as he wiped his face with his napkin and prepared to share Friday evening's events.

"Mrs. Season had an episode during dinner—a medical episode. An ambulance was called, and it appears she had ingested something that made her sick."

"Oh, that's terrible!" Katie, who was seated next to Nash, gasped. "Is she okay?"

"I think so. It certainly added to the very thought-provoking evening and case," Nash admitted. "We are waiting on some results from the lab. Needless to say, it really upset Mrs. Snook."

"Who's she?"

"She is the Season family cook."

"Mrs. Snook, the cook?" Tony laughed uncontrollably. Groans arose from around the table.

"So, how did you get involved, Louie?"

"I was on the north edge of town working on something else, so I wasn't that far away when I heard the call come in. I thought I'd check it out. Since no one knew how she ingested a hallucinogen, it became a police matter."

"What's this case all about anyway? Did she know someone was going to slip her something?" Tony interjected.

"This very rich woman is missing some antiques. She is confident that one of her daughters is the guilty party. I'm supposed to interview them to see if I can determine which one might be the culprit."

"Why doesn't she just ask them?" Tony countered.

"Exactly what I said. Sometimes an outside perspective is more helpful. Anyway, she set up interviews with each of them for me this week."

"Shouldn't that be your call?"

Tony was persistent. His question made Nash a bit uncomfortable, causing him to question his own leniency in the matter. Personally, he would have preferred talking to Giles and Mrs. Snook about the situation in the house first.

"What happens if one of the girls is guilty?" Midge joined in. "Will she turn them over to law enforcement?"

"I don't know; but from what I've seen of Mrs. Season, I wouldn't want to be in that person's shoes."

"Mrs. Season?" Katie quizzed. "Don't you think you are being a bit formal? What's her first name?"

"Tell them, Nash" Anne smiled.

Nash was reluctant.

"Come on, big brother," Tony asked, wondering why Anne was covering a grin. "Is there something else funny about this case? Anne doesn't smile that often. Sorry, Anne."

A second sigh escaped Nash's mouth while Anne gave Tony a disgruntled look.

"Okay, so her name *is* a little strange."

"Don't keep us in suspense," Midge urged.

"All right—her name is Holiday Season," Nash said sheepishly.

"That's funny!" Tony exploded with laughter.

"Wait 'til you hear the rest," Louie added to the story. "There are four beautiful daughters in the family—and I am talking gorgeous! Tell them their names, Nash."

"The four girls are Summer, Winter, Spring, and Autumn," Nash mumbled softly.

"You got to be kidding!" Tony bellowed. "That's rich! Summer Season, Winter Season, Spring Season and Autumn Season! Who would do that to their kids?"

"Apparently, Mr. and Mrs. Season," Midge added, unable to control her giggle.

Tony laughed raucously and slapped the table, causing silverware to clink at the intrusion.

"Anthony!" his mother scolded.

"But it's funny, Ma. Don't you think that's funny? "I suppose the father's name is Hunting or something like that," Tony persisted.

"Actually," Nash said sheepishly, "it's Stormy. Well, that's his nickname anyway."

"You've got to be kidding. You just made that up to embellish the story," Tony said, while Louie raised an eyebrow at the information. He had stayed in the dining room when he had interviewed the family and not examined Mr. Season's portrait.

Nash shook his head.

Ignoring both Louie and her little brother, Midge pushed for more information.

"Maybe it's because of being in the nursing program or maybe because I've learned the suspicious trait from my big brother, but back to this dinner on Friday night—none of the rest of you got sick? You had no reaction to the food?"

"That's right."

"But you all ate the same food, right?"

"As far as I can tell, we all ate the same food."

"You said it was served to you?"

"Yes. There is the cook and a butler, and they served the food and cleared the dishes."

"That's it!" Tony slapped his hands on the table, again. "Mystery solved. The butler did it!"

By that time, Tony's comments were pretty much ignored.

Louie picked up the narrative, explaining that particles of the food left on the plates were examined and nothing was found there or in the kitchen. Samples taken from Mrs. Season's stomach were presently being processed at the local police lab.

"It will take some time for the specific analysis," he concluded. "If our lab doesn't find anything, we will send samples off to the state. In the meantime, we wait. However, the cook was visibly shaken to think that any food she had prepared might have caused the problem."

"So, now I need find out who might be the thief—or maybe an attempted murderer? Or it could be simply a case of some contaminated food. We'll have to wait to see if the incident changes anything."

Nash looked at Louie as if he were asking for help.

"A lot depends on what we find out about what caused the incident with Mrs. Season. It could be something that got there by accident or something that was put there on purpose. If it was on purpose, then we are looking at attempted murder. I have to admit it's a bit suspicious that Holly was targeted since no one else got sick, but it's too early to tell. At this point, it's all speculation."

"So, what are you gonna do, Nash?" Tony asked.

"For now, I intend to proceed just as I was hired to do. I will start interviewing the girls tomorrow per their mother's schedule."

"Per Holiday's request? Are you sure that's wise? What if Mrs. Season faked the whole thing and is just using you to help commit insurance fraud or something?" Anne asked with concern.

"She just had decided which daughter I would interview at which particular time. I will see one daughter on each of the next four afternoons."

"I don't know if I like my big brother being told what to do," Tony was serious. "That doesn't sound like you, Nash."

"I'm not sure I like it either. I am learning things about Holly Season that I may not like, but I'm committed to letting it play out—at least for now."

"Just be cautious, Nash," Katie told him as she placed her hand on his arm. "I wouldn't want anything to happen to you."

"Yep, you know I will be careful," Nash agreed. "Now, what will it be today—volleyball, croquet, or table games? Let's take a break from this case and enjoy the afternoon."

5

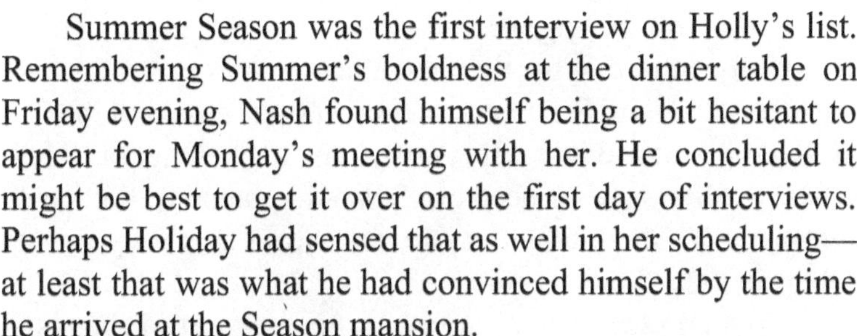

Summer Season was the first interview on Holly's list. Remembering Summer's boldness at the dinner table on Friday evening, Nash found himself being a bit hesitant to appear for Monday's meeting with her. He concluded it might be best to get it over on the first day of interviews. Perhaps Holiday had sensed that as well in her scheduling—at least that was what he had convinced himself by the time he arrived at the Season mansion.

First, he wanted to check to see how Holly was feeling. He found her in the sunroom, reclining on a chaise lounge, reading a book. She took off her reading glasses when she heard Giles greet Nash at the door. As Nash entered the room, she laid her reading glasses and the book she was reading aside.

"So good to see you, Nash," she welcomed but did not offer to move from her position. "I'm so glad you are among those who survived our little dinner party."

"Apparently better than you did," Nash responded. "How are you feeling?"

"Better," she replied. "It was not a pleasant experience, but I managed. Has there been any report on what might have caused it?"

"No. It appears it was some kind of poison, but nothing conclusive as to what. We really won't know anything specific until we get the results from the lab. If our local lab doesn't find anything, we'll send them on to the state, but that will probably take some time. The important thing is that you are feeling better."

Holly reached for a small bell on the table next to her and rang it.

"Thank you. I appreciate your kind words. You are here to meet with Summer, aren't you?"

"Yes, she's the first one on the list you gave to me."

"Be thorough, Nash. Probe. Dig deep. I want to know which one of my daughters is the culprit."

"Don't worry about a thing. You just need to concentrate on feeling better."

Holly smiled at his thoughtfulness.

"You'll find Summer in the potting shed out back," Holly explained as she impatiently rang the bell again. "Now where is Giles when I need him? Would you be so kind as to go by way of the kitchen and to tell Giles I am ready for my afternoon tea?"

"I can do that," Nash told her, heading out of the room in search of Giles.

He encountered Giles in the hallway outside the kitchen.

"Mrs. Season is ready for her tea," he quipped.

"I heard," Giles said dryly.

As Nash continued through the kitchen and out the back door to the potting shed, he mused that Holly Season's impertinence must have rubbed off on the staff.

Once outside, Nash walked into a wonderland of beauty. Flowers of every vibrant color peeked at him from beautifully designed garden beds. Bird baths and fountains and statuary were interspersed. To the far right, beyond a white gazebo, he saw the sparkling waters of a swimming pool. To the left, was a garage that housed several expensive vehicles. He chose to follow one of the walkways that led to a smaller building he guessed must have been the potting shed.

As Nash opened the screen door, he felt the afternoon heat being merely exchanged for the heat of the potting shed. A humming noise from a large stand fan situated in one corner almost masked the sound of music coming from a small radio. The fan's efforts appeared to be successful only at pushing warm air around the room. Shelves were neatly lined with assorted cans, boxes, and flower pots. Debris from plants had been swept into a pile on the floor. Nash observed a door on the far wall which he concluded must lead to a small greenhouse and headed over to it.

As he looked through the greenhouse, he saw a variety of plants situated in the work area as well as soil and garden tools. The opposite end had another door that he assumed led outside. Summer Season stood at a potting table where she was at work planting seedlings. Her back was toward him, so she was not aware of his presence. She wore tan short shorts and a green, plaid blouse that she tied up in front, leaving her midriff bare. Her feet were clad in something resembling combat boots.

She whirled around when she realized she was not alone. The sun from a nearby window spread its light across her short blonde hair. She reached up to her forehead to push an unruly curl back into place and left a smudge instead. In that brief moment, Nash thought about how much Summer reflected her name. She was like a ray of sunshine.

"Oh, hello, Nash!" she smiled sweetly, and Nash's stomach suddenly relived the foot incident at Friday evening's dinner.

"Hello, Summer," he smiled uncomfortably. "At least we have that much out of the way. We both remember each other's names."

Instead of verbally responding, she removed her gloves and gestured toward a high stool. He pulled it a little farther away from the one she chose. In response to his move, she batted her eyes and shook her head. She had to stretch to sit on the seat and used the potting table to help her adjust. She propped one foot on the rung of the stool and crossed her smooth, long, tan legs. Nash could not help but notice her slender legs and ankles.

"I know why you're here," she said impatiently. "Holiday has briefed us all. Take as long as you like. I have all afternoon and can think of no other way I'd like to spend it than with a handsome guy."

Again, she smiled at him and Nash blushed. She was not going to make this easy.

"I just need to get to know you better—" he began and then regretted phrasing the statement that way.

"I'd like to get to know you better, as well," Summer said with a grin and attempted to scoot closer to him.

"Not like that," Nash said, recovering his voice and pushing away while the beautiful Summer stuck out her bottom lip in a pretend pout.

"This is purely business," he continued. "Can you think of anyone who would want to steal from your mother?"

"Almost anyone I know," she sighed. "Holiday has not made it easy for anyone she's ever come in contact with as you may have observed at the dinner Friday night. She is demanding, cruel, and sarcastic and just plain mean at times. To hear her tell it, we are all a disappointment to her."

"How would you say you have disappointed your mother?"

"Really, Nash? I am a glorified gardener, a position that does not measure up to Holiday Season's expectations. I am twenty years old and should be traveling in circles where I can meet wealthy young men according to her. Instead, I play in the dirt. What a disappointment I must surely be."

Disregarding her outburst, Nash struggled to continue.

"Where were you on the night of July 10th?"

"You certainly do get right to the point," Summer smiled. "It just so happens that I was having dinner at the Coral Room."

"Alone?"

"No. Actually, it was a date."

"So, this date could verify the information?"

"I'd rather you didn't talk with him. Conrad turned out to be a jerk. I'd just as soon not be linked to him ever again. But, now, our waiter, Rene, well, there's someone I'm sure would remember me. You can talk to him. He can tell you what you need to know."

"You were there all evening?"

"As I said, Conrad turned out to be a bore. I'd say we got there about 7:00, and I was back here by 10:00 or so—after Rene and I got to know each other." Her smile was wicked.

"Did you see anything suspicious when you returned here?"

"No. All was quiet—except for Winter. She was still up and about."

Nash nodded as he jotted down some notes.

"What do you make of what happened at the dinner on Friday—your mother getting sick and all?"

"I've never seen Holiday out of control of a situation. That was a surprise. Poisoned? Intentionally? I can think of a hundred reasons why it could happen—but I can't think of any one of us actually doing it."

"So, you're responsible for all the beautification on the property?" Nash changed the subject.

"Exactly."

"That's amazing, Summer! The flowers are spectacular. You definitely have a knack for working with plants, flowers, and landscape design."

"Thank you."

"Makes me wonder what it's like around here at Christmastime."

"Oh, I decorate everything outside—Christmas or, well, look at these plans. I've been working on these for this coming season. Maybe you can visit at Christmastime," she suggested with a smirk.

But Summer became serious about her work as she cleared a space on the potting bench and spread some papers out in front of them. Nash stood from his seat to study them. Summer narrated while Nash perused the sketches.

"Summer, these are indeed impressive. You are very talented!"

"Thank you," she said as she once again rolled the plans and slipped a rubber band around them.

"How did you ever get interested in something like this?"

"I guess when I was about twelve years old. I was at the library, and I saw some photos there. Do you remember the old depot downtown at the train station? Well, back in the day, it was a really nice place for weary train travelers to rest on their journey. There was a small restaurant nearby where passengers could get food, and a hotel within walking distance. But the gardens were the main attraction. I mean, the railroad went all out to hire gardeners to make it special. There were benches placed among the flowers for those who had packed a lunch or just wanted to enjoy the outdoors after spending hours on the noisy train. Anyway, the gardens were amazingly beautiful. I guess I just wanted to create something like those."

Nash began to see Summer in a little different light.

"Did you ever want to do anything else with your life?"

"Not really. When father was alive, he encouraged us all to pursue whatever we wanted to do. Of course, it helps that money was never an issue. Now, Holiday has each of us on a budget," she stopped long enough to roll her beautiful brown eyes. "And going over budget is a crime around here."

"Do you go over budget? And what is the penalty for going over budget?"

"Of course, I go over budget," Summer said as she hopped down from her perch. "If for no other reason than to see Holiday fly into a rage. She seldom does anything other than spout off at the mouth and belittle us. It's become a game of sorts."

Nash watched Summer as she continued her potting. In the silence that followed, he looked around the room. He noticed all the pesticides and other chemicals that were stored there. Certainly, the potting shed was a good source of poisonous materials.

"Surely you don't do all this work yourself."

Summer's eyes grew big. "Of course not," she said, resuming her playful attitude. "I have two, twenty-year-old guys who come here twice a week. They are well-built and extremely good looking, and I force them to work shirtless. I would not accept anything less."

Nash was once again embarrassed by her brashness.

"I'm lying," she laughed as her eyes twinkled with mischief. "I have an older man who is sixty something. He comes twice a week and sometimes brings his twelve-year-old grandson."

She giggled while Nash attempted to regain his composure.

"You are so gullible, Nash," Summer teased. "That surprises me."

"You're the youngest daughter, right?" Nash asked, ignoring Summer's comment and attempting to change the subject.

"Yes. I'm twenty."

"I repeat: It's amazing what you've done here with the flowers and landscaping—and only twenty years old."

"How old are you, Nash?" she asked as she leaned closer to him.

"Older than twenty," he smiled.

"I'm guessing twenty-five."

"You might be correct," he pretended.

"You're not too old," she winked.

"Summer, you are something else. I am here to glean information."

"Here's some information for you. There hasn't been a male come to this house who can measure up to Holiday's standards for us, and I don't suppose there ever will be."

Nash almost felt sorry for the young lady in front of him and struggled to remain professional.

"If you thought one of your sisters could be guilty of the theft, which one would you think it would be?"

Summer paused.

"Probably Autumn. She resents Holiday maybe more than the rest of us."

"Because?"

"Because she's the biggest disappointment."

"How so?"

"An artist? Really, Nash. That ranks right up there with being a gardener. But, seriously, I'm not sure why Holiday comes down so hard on Autumn's choice of profession. My sister creates some good work."

Nash considered all the things Summer had said, some believable and some not so believable. He thought it was fruitless to continue questioning her for now.

"Thanks, Summer. You've been a big help."

"I have, haven't I?" she said playfully but then became serious. "I know what Holiday suspects, but, Mr. Adams—none of my sisters is guilty of taking her antiques. You can search the premises if you like. I'd even help you. Besides what would be the point for one of us to have done it? It will all belong to the four of us one day anyway."

"Thanks again," Nash said as he gave Summer one of his cards before leaving the potting shed and the beautiful Summer.

Thoughts raced through Nash's mind as he drove back to town. It was clear that Summer resented her mother, but was that resentment deep enough to steal or perhaps harm her? One thing was for sure, there was more to Summer Season than a flirtatious young woman. He made note of the chemicals in the potting shed and the fact that Summer invariably spoke of her mother by her first name.

As was his habit with each of his cases, Nash was busy creating a wall of information on the office wall when Anne came in after lunch. Putting the information on the wall where he could see it all at one time helped Nash organize and sort through it. As each important fact was discovered, he added it to the wall.

"My goodness, that is a beautiful young woman," Anne exclaimed as she noticed Summer's photo tacked to the wall. "One interview down?"

Nash nodded his head.

"Productive?"

"Not much," he answered as he used a marker to write some facts on a paper tacked under Summer's photo. "She is the youngest of the Season girls and a gardener of sorts. She has done some beautiful landscaping on the property."

"But...? There seems to be more."

"I don't know. She doesn't seem like she'd take the antiques. I just can't get a handle on it, yet. If she had anything to do with poisoning her mother, it escapes me although she certainly had the opportunity—and the means. The potting shed is filled with all kinds of poisonous chemicals.”

“It’s probably too soon to draw conclusions,” Anne wisely advised. “Besides, there’s a lot more interviewing to be done. Who’s next on Holly’s list?”

“Spring. She’s the nurse.”

## 6

Temperatures continued to soar as Nash arrived promptly on Tuesday afternoon for his interview with Spring.

"Spring just sent me a text. She is running late," Holly was clearly irritated as she explained the situation. "Apparently, there was some emergency at the hospital."

Nash nodded in response to the information. Although Nash had found Holly in the sun room again, she was no longer confined to the chaise lounge. As a matter of fact, she seemed to have made a full recovery.

"How did it go yesterday? With Summer, that is?" Holly inquired.

"Umm, not that I want to keep anything from you, but I am still in the process of acquiring information. I really don't have anything to discuss right now. It's too soon. Can you understand that?"

Nash was almost fearful that Holly would react badly to his opinion, but she did not. Instead, she indicated that she understood—taking him by surprise. It would appear the Season household held many surprises.

The doorbell rang, and Giles seemed to appear from nowhere and immediately rushed past the sun room. His entrance was so quick and abrupt that Nash considered the fact he might have been eavesdropping on their conversation.

"Mr. Wainwright," Giles announced upon his return.

"Show him in," Holly responded.

"Walter Wainwright, I'd like for you to meet Nash Adams. Mr. Adams is doing some work for me concerning the theft. Nash, this is Walter Wainwright, my attorney."

The two men were exchanging pleasantries just as Spring arrived.

"I'll meet you at the gazebo out beyond the back of the house," she said, after looking disconcerted at Mr. Wainwright's presence. "I want to change clothes before we talk—if you don't mind. It's been a long day. I'll stop off in the kitchen and get us something cool to drink before heading out there."

Nash found his way to the gazebo by following the carefully placed garden stepping stone path as he had been instructed to do. Once there he found a commanding view of the property. He was not a connoisseur of flowers, but he recognized many different varieties from his mother's yard and from his grandmother's garden. There were patches of multi-colored zinnias, golden and orange marigolds, talk stalks of hollyhocks, Russian lavender, rows of colorful snapdragons, and yellow and white daisies. Pink begonias with glossy bright green leaves lined the walkways while clumps of chrysanthemums waited next to them for their turn at bloom. Sturdy sunflowers turning their faces to the sun peeked above the small greenhouse in the distance. Roses in brilliant colors of deep reds and pastel pinks and brilliant oranges and delicate yellows surrounded a bird bath. Several carefully selected statuaries were placed thoughtfully and strategically throughout the garden. All that Nash saw he attributed to Summer's creativity and hard work.

Nash found the face-to-face wooden glider in the gazebo to be soothing as well as unique. He leaned back and closed his eyes. The July heat was relentless and sapped energy from anyone with the slightest movement. It was relaxing just to sit there and enjoy the slight breeze the glider created. He finally opened his eyes and was startled to find out he was not alone. Summer, dressed in jean shorts and a skimpy top, stood near the one side of the gazebo. He startled.

"My, you *are* a jumpy one," she giggled.

"I wasn't expecting to see you," Nash said as he cleared his throat. "Your day was yesterday."

"But I might have more information," she pouted.

"Do you?"

"Well, no," she laughed. "But I could make something up."

"I'm only interested in the facts."

"Hmm," Summer frowned. "Nevertheless, I like you anyway."

"Did you come out here on purpose to snoop? This is Spring's day."

"No, I just saw you over here. I was working on the riding mower and couldn't pass up the opportunity," she laughed.

It was then Nash noticed the screwdriver in her hand and the smudge of motor oil on her face.

"Are you telling me you work on gardening equipment as well?"

"Seems like it comes with the job. Anyway, I like repairing things."

Just then, Spring emerged from the house and made her way to the gazebo, so Summer returned to the potting shed after a quick smile and wave to Nash.

"Just ignore her," Spring said. "She's a handful, but she's generally harmless."

Nash was not sure he totally agreed with Spring's assessment that her sister was harmless and could not think of an appropriate reply so he remained quiet. He noted that Spring had indeed made a change from hospital garb into pale blue shorts, a white tank top, and sandals. She had clipped her light brown hair to the top of her head. As she sat down across from him on the glider, she kicked off her sandals as soon.

"I hope you like root beer," she said, offering him one of the delightfully frosty bottles.

"Anything cold," Nash replied. "This heat is really hanging on."

"Yes, we've had a lot of weather-related cases at the hospital."

The wooden glider creaked when Spring started the gentle back and forth movement.

"This is really neat," he observed. "I haven't seen one of these in a long time."

"It's one of Summer's innovations," Spring explained. "I assume she saw one somewhere and then designed this one for here. This is actually one of my favorite places."

"I can see why."

"On your feet a lot?" Nash dipped his chin toward the discarded sandals.

"Oh, yes! I don't think I sat down at all today. Plus, we're shorthanded, and I've put in some extra hours this week. It's good to just relax a bit." A troubled look flitted across her face. Then, she sighed as she closed her eyes and held the cold bottle to her forehead to relieve the tension stored there.

"I suspect you are good at your job."

"Thanks. I like to think so. Most patients are very easy to work with. But there are always those few..." her voice trailed off.

"I can imagine. Would you classify your mother as one of *those few?*"

"That's very astute of you, Mr. Adams," she smiled. "Yes, my mother is not the ideal patient—or the ideal mother, for that matter."

"Why is that? She seems to be intelligent, and I think almost caring on some level."

"I suppose that's the key—on some level. If it is there, it hardly ever struggles to the surface. But why isn't she ideal? I've thought about that a lot. She is entirely different from our father. He was kind and generous and encouraging. He came from money. Mother did not. I think that's the problem. She never had things growing up, so she covets social status, money, and control."

"She surely is proud of you, being a nurse and all. That's an admirable profession."

"Hardly," Spring scoffed. "Now, if I had become a doctor, that would have been different. Being a doctor would carry more prestige. But not a nurse. No way! I have been reminded of that frequently."

"I'm sorry," Nash murmured, overlooking the bitterness he detected in Spring's voice. "It must be difficult under those circumstances. But you must view being a nurse as very rewarding."

"It is. It's what I've wanted to do since I was a little girl."

Nash noted the wistfulness in her voice. Spring was no less attractive than her other sisters. He guessed the caring he saw in her large blue eyes was an asset when dealing with hospital patients.

"Why do you continue to live here? After all, you could be independent, couldn't you? I mean, you make enough as a nurse to support yourself."

"Financially, yes. But independent? Not exactly. Our mother told us we are all bound by some mysterious clause in our father's will, one that prohibits us from leaving this house permanently until the youngest daughter turns twenty-five years old—or until our mother dies. Something to do with being disinherited. I guess none of us really wants that—although it's not about the money."

Nash hoped his face did not reflect the feeling in the pit of his stomach. He looked into Spring's eyes and saw the sadness there.

"Still, that could be a reason for poisoning your mother. Which one of your sisters do you think could be capable of such a thing?"

"Actually, none of them. There's no doubt that we all would stand to gain if something happened to her–especially Summer with her being the youngest and knowing that twenty-five is the magic number. Five years is a long time for someone who is impatient. Winter also would gain much. She will be past thirty by then. A lot of life can pass you by the time you're thirty."

"Is there no way of changing your mother's mind about that?"

"Mr. Adams, you've met my mother, right?"

Nash nodded. He was beginning to realize that things were even more complicated than he first thought.

"Were you at the hospital the night of July 10th?"

"As a matter of fact, I was. My shift finished about 6:00, but I met a co-worker for dinner. I got back here about 9:00 or so. And before you ask, I didn't see anyone else except for Winter who had gone for a swim in the pool."

"Does she do that often?"

"It's not unusual. Winter is an accomplished swimmer and often swims at night. She finds it relaxing."

"So, this co-worker you had dinner with? They could verify you were there?"

"Yes, of course. Nash, I would do anything to help if it means making my family the happy family it used to be."

"One more question—Summer made some comment about young men coming here and not measuring up to your mother's standards. Do you share that opinion?"

"It's quite true. That's why none of us ever bring our male friends here anymore. The guy I had dinner with? He works at the hospital. But he's a lab technician—not a doctor. If he were a doctor, I suppose that would impress mother. To be honest, Nash, all of us tend to keep things from our mother. It's just easier that way."

Nash nodded and stood to leave.

"Thanks for the root beer," he told her. "And thanks for your time. Here's my card. You can call that number any time if you think of anything else."

Nash left the Season estate with questions still unanswered. Both Summer and Spring seemed open to his questions. Neither acted as if they were guilty. However, one big unanswered question stared him in the face: What was Mr. Wainwright's frequent business with Holiday Season?

Nash dropped by the precinct on his way home after his interview with Spring. He always enjoyed talking to Louie, but he was hoping there would be some news from the crime lab. He bounded up the stone steps of the old landmark building with the massive oak doors. He was glad the city had decided to keep the old building as well as the statue that stood before it of one of the early founders of Mason County. Preserving history was a love he shared with his sister, Midge.

Once inside the building, several employees greeted Nash's familiar face. The temperature inside was only slightly cooler than outside, but despite the heat, Nash chose the stairs rather than the elevator. Three flights of stairs later he was weaving through the maze of desks to Louie's corner station.

As usual, Louie was on the telephone, and his desk was buried under piles of file folders. Nash could not remember ever seeing it in any other condition. Louie was not known for his neatness. Plastic coffee cups and empty food containers crept over the side of the overflowing waste basket. Nash firmly believed Sunday dinners at the Adams' house were probably the only times he ate a home-cooked meal.

"Hey, pull up a chair," Louie welcomed him as he hung up the telephone and pushed his chair back from the congested desk. "What brings you downtown?"

"I just came from my interview with Spring Season, so I thought I'd swing by to see if you've heard anything yet about the poisoning."

"It's probably too soon. They said they were backed up, so I don't expect to hear anything for a while."

Nash nodded.

"You want some coffee?"

"Nah. Too hot."

"You got that right. This heat drains the life right out of a fella. As you can tell, the AC's not keeping up with this. I just hope the grid doesn't go down with all the extra demand."

"That would be disaster. I heard this morning the heat was supposed to last three more days."

"Brutal!" Louie said. "You say you've started the interviews? How's that goin'? You found out anything that might be helpful?"

"Not yet. I've interviewed Summer and Spring. They are a lot more complicated than I first thought. It seems they all could have motive. Their mother seems to control them as well as the finances. Summer does gardening for the household and has access to a lot of poisonous materials. Spring is a nurse, so she would have access to drugs. Either one could have slipped something into their mother's food before it was brought into the dining room."

Just then the telephone rang, and Louie rushed to answer it. The call was brief.

"Sorry. That was the lab. They are still working on their analysis. Whatever poison it is, it is not common. They have ruled out all of those. They are going to send samples to the state lab."

"Hmm," Nash frowned.

"We'll get to the bottom of it," Louie assured him as Nash stood to leave.

"Hey, do you know anything about a Walter Wainwright? He's an attorney—Holly Season's attorney, to be exact."

"Name's not familiar to me," Louie said, shaking his head. "Spelling?"

Louie jotted the name down on a piece of paper while Nash spelled it.

"I'll ask around," Louie promised.

Nash left, wondering how the tiny piece of paper Louie used could survive on the desk long enough for him to check out the name.

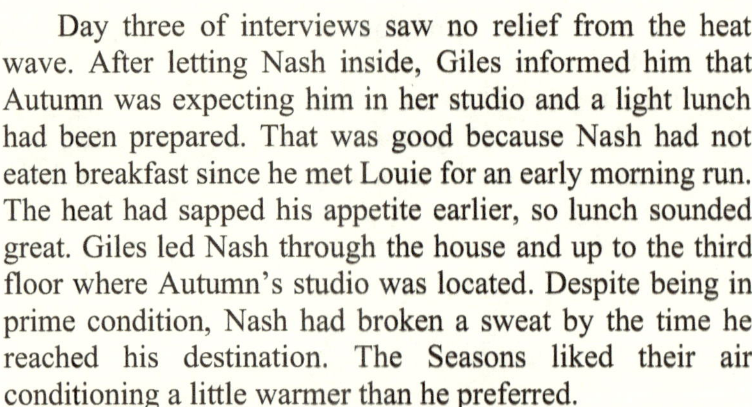

## 7

Day three of interviews saw no relief from the heat wave. After letting Nash inside, Giles informed him that Autumn was expecting him in her studio and a light lunch had been prepared. That was good because Nash had not eaten breakfast since he met Louie for an early morning run. The heat had sapped his appetite earlier, so lunch sounded great. Giles led Nash through the house and up to the third floor where Autumn's studio was located. Despite being in prime condition, Nash had broken a sweat by the time he reached his destination. The Seasons liked their air conditioning a little warmer than he preferred.

All of the bedrooms in the Season house were located on the second floor. The third floor housed three things: Autumn's art studio, a storage room, and Winter's writing den. He found Autumn waiting for him.

Once again, Nash was overwhelmed by Autumn's beauty. Her auburn hair was pulled back into a pony tail. He noted that even her coloring reflected the colors of her name. She wore sage green shorts and a shirt splashed with rust, orange, and the same hue of green from the shorts. She greeted him with a friendly smile. Her doe eyes were beguiling.

"Won't you have a seat?" she asked as she gestured to a straight chair that she obviously had artistically painted with colorful flowers. "There's bottled water."

"Thanks," Nash replied as he became conscious of the perspiration running down his face. "It's another hot one out there again."

Giles appeared with a tray of food. Nash startled at his entrance. There was something eerie about the way the butler appeared and disappeared without a sound. Nash decided he was glad he could not afford servants.

"Will that be all, Miss?" The trek up the steps had winded the small and somewhat elderly man, and he paused to wipe his balding head.

"Yes. Thank you, Giles."

Giles vanished as silently as he had appeared while Autumn uncovered a lunch comprised of tiny crustless sandwiches and assorted fruit.

"Help yourself," she encouraged.

Nash was more than happy to do so as he took in the ambiance of the room. It was what one would expect from an artist's pad. The room was rather large, stretching the entire width of the house. Natural light penetrated from windows on the east, the west, the south, and from a glass dome in the ceiling. Two photography lights were at the ready to create shadows or more lighting if needed. There were several easels of various sizes with partially finished drawings on them. Paint brushes were perched inside jars of liquid.

Several paintings were displayed on the walls, most of them sceneries. Some were florals, and Nash noticed a bouquet of dead flowers in a wastebasket that must have recently been the subject of a painting. There were water colors, oils, acrylics, charcoal and pencil drawings. Obviously, Autumn was not limited to one medium.

Although Nash did not consider himself a connoisseur of art, he thought Autumn was very good at her craft. He was intrigued by a series of black and white sketches which Nash thought were inked self-portraits. The subject was dressed in a variety of clothing, but her face was never visible, always concealed by a hand, a fan, a flower.

One, in particular caught his eye. In it, she wore a man's sport coat, and a fedora-style hat shielded her face. A second drawing in a rather prominent position also caught his attention. It was a rather large canvas done in charcoal. The subject was a man who seemed familiar. He noted that it was the only framed picture in the gallery.

"I see you have met my father," Autumn said when she noticed his attention to it.

"That is the same man in the painting above the fireplace in the sun room," Nash observed.

"Yes. However, my mother commissioned the downstairs painting by a professional."

Nash could hear the resentment in her voice. Her emphasis on the word "commissioned" reflected her displeasure.

"Somehow, I think you've caught something special in this one, something the one above the fireplace lacks."

"Thank you, Nash," she said, her face softening. "That's a great compliment to an aspiring artist."

"These sandwiches are good," he said, diverting her attention from a touchy subject.

Autumn smiled. "I would tell you I made them myself, but anyone is this household will tell you that I do nothing except my art—a silly and selfish adventure."

"Why do you say that about yourself? You obviously have talent."

"Well, not to hear the one and only Holiday Season tell it. According to her, it is a foolish waste of time and will never afford me the opportunity to be independent."

"Is that what you want—to be independent?"

"All I care about is creating what I see in the world and what I feel in here," she said as she patted her chest.

"I would think these paintings alone would sell for quite a price," Nash said as he waved his hand toward her work. "Of course, I only like what I see. I have no background in art."

"If ever they were sold."

"You mean you don't sell your work?"

"No. I guess I just have never dealt with the commercial part of it all."

Nash was quiet as he once again took in the scope of what the room had to offer. Finally, he decided to ask the question that had been bothering him since they talked about the drawing of her father.

"Have you any drawings of your mother?"

"Oh, yes," she said as she got to her feet and sorted through some canvases. "Somewhere around here."

She finally pulled two small sheets of art paper, smaller than anything else Nash had seen in the room and presented them to him. They were done in pencil. Each one was unique, displaying two different sides of Holly. In the one, she almost appeared to be the loving mother. In the other, she portrayed the demanding person Nash had observed.

"These are—," Nash was at a loss for words.

"Are the same woman?" Autumn finished his thought as she took the pictures from his hands and put them back behind the others. "Yes, they are both Holiday Season. I call them *The Before and After Duo.*"

Nash frowned in confusion.

"Present day and the way she used to be," Autumn explained.

"Are you saying that Holly was a more loving mother at one time?"

Autumn sat down with a sigh. When she looked into Nash's eyes with her soft brown ones, he thought he might have detected a tear.

"Maybe. But that's so far back, I surely am mistaken," she said pensively. "Now, Mr. Adams, about this visit. Just what do you expect to garnish from a conversation with an unknown artist?"

"As an artist, are you interested in antiques?"

"You're asking me if I've taken the items from the house. No, I haven't. Nor do I believe my sisters have either."

"Do you have any ideas about anyone who might want to hurt your mother?"

"Perhaps everyone. But certainly no one in this house."

"Has anyone else had access to the house? I mean anyone who could quite possibly have contaminated any of the food."

"I seldom leave this attic room, so I have little opportunity to observe anyone who comes and goes. You can ask any of my sisters to verify that. Art is my life. I do not observe life with the perimeters other people use to define it. I'm sorry I can't be of more help to you."

Nash nodded his head and sat quietly for a time. Then he stood and walked around the room, again, looking for anything he might have missed. He paused to look through the east windows, overlooking the back yard and its beauty. From that view, one could observe Summer's master plan for the estate's yard. Here it was equally as impressive as it had been the previous day from the gazebo. He saw the pool, the potting shed, the greenhouse, the garages, and another small building.

"What is that little building beyond the greenhouse?" he asked.

"Oh, that's Giles' place. He's been in that little house for as long as I can remember."

"He's been with the family a long time?"

"Oh, yes," she nodded. "Probably 40 years or so. He was here when my grandparents were alive. And before my parents were married. He's a permanent fixture around here."

Nash nodded, continuing his journey across the well-stained drop cloth on the floor through the maze of canvases and partially finished works of art.

"I'm still curious," he finally stated. "I would think you would be interested in sharing your accomplishments with the world."

"Maybe," she said thoughtfully. "Maybe—someday. Sometimes I think about having my own small gallery."

"There's a room at the library," Nash was excited at the prospect. "They often use it to display various local talent—everything from crafts to authors to musicians. I think they would be open and very excited to host a viewing for you. It's none of my business—I know. But I think you are talented. Others should know about your work. You might even find a buyer or two. Well, it's something for you to think about anyway."

"I thought you were here to find Holiday's antiques—not to give business advice," Autumn's voice was strained. Nash decided he had enough information from her.

"Here's my card. Give me a call if you think of anything that might help in the investigation."

Autumn took the card. Nash hoped it would not end up with the dead flowers in the wastebasket. He felt as if the interview had come to a rather abrupt end, but he also felt that perhaps he had overstepped with his enthusiasm for a public display of Autumn's art work.

Just as he turned to leave, Autumn called after him.

"Oh, Nash, would you sit for me sometime? You have some features I'd like to capture on canvas."

"I think you can find better subjects than me," he replied and hurried down the stairs.

Autumn was certainly different from her sisters. Nash felt a connection with her. Of all the observations he made, the one that stood out most to him was the contrast between Autumn's artistic rendering of her father and the renderings of her mother. The father's portrait was rather large and placed in a position of prominence on the wall while Holly's were small pencil drawings, hidden out of sight. A psychiatrist would have a field day with that. One thing was for sure—Autumn Season was lost in her world of art, seeing things in life others missed while missing the things others saw.

8

←——————————————————→

"Miss Winter is still in the pool," Giles announced as Nash, adhering to Holly Season's schedule, made his appearance on Thursday to question the final Season daughter. "Shall I summon her, or do you prefer to meet with her out there?"

"I'll go to her," Nash agreed, thinking the elderly Giles certainly looked tired.

The pool sounded like a great idea on such a warm day, and Nash momentarily wished he was taking advantage of a cool swim. Upon his arrival on the cement pool deck, Nash watched Winter as her lithe body sprang from the diving board. Her slender figure cut perfectly through the water. She saw him just as she surfaced and waved to him.

"Want to go for a swim?" she shouted, reaching up to brush her wet hair from her face.

"Can't," Nash replied, knowing he would enjoy nothing more on such a warm day. "I'm working."

He heard the sparkle in her laughter at his remark.

"I just have two more laps to go," she said, "if you don't mind."

"Sure. Go ahead."

Nash made himself comfortable in a lounge chair under one of the poolside umbrellas. He tried to take in the surroundings, but he could not keep his eyes from the figure in the blue swim suit. Even that seemed to match the color of the pool's liner.

Winter was a good swimmer. She finished the two laps rather quickly and emerged from the pool dripping with water.

"Towel," she requested, pointing to a nearby chair.

Nash retrieved the towel and tossed it to her.

"Thanks," she said. "I didn't want to get you all wet by coming closer. Do you swim?"

"Yeah, I guess I'm pretty fair at swimming. But then, I've never had a pool in my backyard, so I suspect you are better than me."

"We'll have to test that someday. I'll go change and meet you up in my writing room—if that's okay with you."

He nodded and followed her to the house. She walked in front of him, towel tied around her body which was still dripping water. When they came to the second floor where the bedrooms were located, she told him she would not be long and parted ways with him. He continued up the last flight of stairs alone.

The writing nook was an interesting room, much smaller than the art room. Light from a small dormer cast a stream of light across the room. To his left as he entered was a tier of shelves filled with books and notebooks that extended behind the edge of a large desk situated diagonally across the far corner of the room. An assortment of blue and white flowers nestled among feathery greenery in a rather large vase occupied one side of the desk.

Nash moved closer for a more thorough investigation. The surface of the desk contained a laptop and several notepads and papers strewn about in an only slightly more organized mess than what he had seen on Louie's desk. A mug containing pens and pencils and a couple of picture frames were situated under the desk lamp. Picking up one of the notepads, he read notes about what he decided must have been ideas for a mystery Winter was writing. After scanning a few more pages, he put it back in its place, deciding that Winter did have a way with words.

Nash tenderly picked up a 5" x 7" photo. Four little girls wearing cute frilly dresses and huge smiles peered back at him. Obviously, these were the Season sisters—Summer with a head full of blonde curls, a rather shy Spring, the dark serious eyes of Autumn, and the haunting ones of Winter. He estimated their ages to be two through six or so. He returned the picture frame to its place. On the opposite side of the desk near the bouquet of flowers he noticed a tiny folding picture frame which contained two photos. He recognized the young couple as Holly and her husband.

Glancing at the rest of the room from this angle, he immediately became distracted by an entire wall of framed photographs. It looked as if they had been taken on some kind of trip or safari. He moved to the wall and was so intent on looking at them that he was not aware of Winter's presence.

"Ah, are you interested in travel, Mr. Adams?" she asked as she joined him.

"Oh, well, yes," he replied.

The aroma of her perfume began surrounding him. He looked into her sparkling eyes peering curiously at him from her gorgeous face. For a brief moment, he pondered the thought of how one family could have been blessed with so many beautiful women. Winter was the tallest of the four girls and more athletic in build. She had changed into a pair of white shorts and sandals with a blue and silver polo shirt. Her dark hair was still damp from the swim. She appeared pleasantly cool reminding him of the first time Holly had appeared in his office.

"These are very interesting. Africa?" he asked, returning his attention to the photos.

"Yes," she confirmed. "I was sent there to do some research for an article I was writing.

"This was our campsite, and this one is of me with our native guide and our interpreter," she said as she began a tour of the photos. "This is me with some of the native women and children who live there. Oh, and this is a photo of our means of transportation. And this one is of our photographer. This is us ready to leave on a hunting expedition. Believe me, all of these people became very special—and necessary—to me."

He could tell by the tone of her voice that she was passionate about the trip. There was also a hint of caring when she talked about the women and children.

"That must have been an exciting trip."

"Very. I learned a lot. I also learned that I'm not cut out for living in the jungles or for being hot and sweaty. The closest thing to a pool was a muddy river teeming with all kinds of disgusting looking creatures."

Nash laughed at her remark. "When were these taken?"

"Just a couple of months ago. I've been back less than a month now."

"Oh, so these are fairly recent then. Did you see lots of animals?" He asked standing in front of a photo of a herd of zebras.

"Yes. Quite a few. This picture is not very clear, but if you look closely, you can see a family of elephants just near those trees." Winter pointed to an area near the horizon. "We were encouraged to keep our distance—something I didn't need to be reminded of more than once. One day, we came upon a pride of lions almost before we knew it. When the male lion looked our direction and shook his shaggy head, I was quite ready to get out of there. We did go hunting one day but not for sport. It was because the people in the village needed food."

Her eyes reflected some degree of sadness in her last remark.

"I take it food was an issue there?" he commented.

"It seemed to me that their entire existence was about obtaining enough food to stay alive. We don't often think of things like that in our society. Each day for them was about making it through to the next with very little hope for the future."

There was a long pause while both digested that comment.

"How long were you there?"

"The entire trip took over a month. We were basically with one tribe back in the interior for about two weeks. The rest of the time was travel. I took tons of notes on their lifestyle—eating habits, ways of surviving the weather, hunting, gardening, medical practices, uses of plants and animals from their environment—those sorts of things. The experience was quite different from anything I had ever undergone before."

"And could I say lifechanging?"

Winter nodded. "Lifechanging. I fear I have left some of my heart there with the natives, especially the children," she added wistfully. "The people were so poor! Each day was about survival for them. They had never known anything beyond their small village. And the children! So precious, so innocent!"

"Sounds like you have a rewarding profession," Nash said, clearing his throat and changing the subject. "You probably are paid well for your talent."

"Well, it could be if it was regular. But these assignments are few and far between making the overall amount I earn unsubstantial—so it's not very lucrative."

After a few more quiet minutes of studying the photos together, Winter invited Nash to have a seat. She chose the chair behind the desk for herself and unconsciously rearranged papers.

"I know you are here because of our mother," she began, "but I honestly don't know what I can tell you. I don't know anything about her antiques, and she is what she is: demanding, uncompromising, controlling, and a lot of other unpleasant things. My first impulse last week when she became ill was that she was pretending. She does things sometimes to get attention." Winter leaned forward intensely as if gathering information for one of her stories and asked in a hushed voice "Have there been any new developments with the laboratory results?"

"No. Although they established that it was indeed poison, they haven't been able to identify it beyond the fact that it was something rare."

Winter's eyes returned to the photos on the wall and then quickly looked away.

"I wish I could help you, Nash, but I don't know how something could have gotten into the food. None of the rest of us got sick. I'm pretty sure my sisters were not involved. Oh, I know we all have reason enough, but I don't think any of us would go to such lengths."

"How about the missing articles from the house?"

"Beats me. Again, I don't think any of us girls would have been involved. We have our monthly allowances, which are sufficient. It just doesn't make sense. It would be like stealing from ourselves."

"What do you know about the stipulations in your father's will?" Nash approached the subject.

"That's something I've never quite understood," Winter frowned. "If you had known my father, you would think that such a thing would not be possible for him to have included in his will. He was a kind and generous man, not controlling. His requirement seems out of character to me. However, if my mother had anything to do with that decision, I can't come up with a reason why. I've approached mother several times about it but to no avail. She is very secretive about it. Mr. Wainwright, however, has confirmed that everything mother says is true. I even asked to see a copy of the will once."

"And did you see it?'

"No. I think it was about the time something else came up in the family that required my attention, and it was soon forgotten."

"But you are receiving an adequate allowance? All of you?"

"Well, adequate barely covers it. It's not like we're starving or anything. It's just enough to keep us humble, though."

"What about the missing antiques?"

"What would be the reason for one of us to have stolen them? It doesn't make any sense. Everything in this house will be ours one day."

"Maybe one of you can't wait that long. You might be planning to elope before the will says you can."

"Restricting our residence to this home doesn't mean we don't have lives outside these acres. No, the only reason I can think one of us might have taken them is out of revenge for mother's domineering ways. But that could be a reason for any of us to have done it."

"How long has it been since your father passed away?"

"Three years. That's when this all began with mother—her hardness, her obsession with money. Perhaps it has more to do with his death. I really don't know. I know that she makes all of us uncomfortable, now. Nash, we used to be a family—a happy family. Now we don't talk; we don't communicate. It's like something was ripped from us when our father died."

"I'm sorry," he murmured when he was certain she was finished talking.

Winter brushed a tear from her eyes and shook her head as if to clear it of recent thoughts. Nash chose to lighten the conversation.

"What are your aspirations? With your writing and all?"

Winter leaned back in the chair with a sigh. "Someday, I want to become the published author of a first-class novel," she smiled at the thought.

"So how is that going?"

"Look for yourself," Winter laughed as she gestured towards the shelves. "See those folders? Each one contains the ingredients for a best-seller."

Nash studied Winter's beautiful face. Of all the Season women, Winter was an odd mixture of strength and compassion. Being the oldest, she obviously assumed the role of protecting her sisters. Nash wondered if she would go so far as to protect someone who was guilty of a crime.

Nash rose and looked once more at the pictures from the African trip. Then he moved to the window. It was the same view he had witnessed from the window in Autumn's art studio.

"Is that a surveillance camera?" he asked.

"Where?" Winter was by his side suddenly, and her closeness disturbed him.

"There. It looks like some kind of camera on the side of the greenhouse."

"Oh, that. That's Summer's doing. She likes to keep track of animals that attack her plants in the middle of the night."

"Does it work?"

"I really don't know."

"Speaking of cameras, is there one on the front gates or are they always open?"

"We don't have a camera that I know of. The gate is generally locked unless we are expecting someone. We all have devices so it's never a problem."

"When you came home the night of the 10th, was the gate open or closed?"

Winter turned from the window.

"Now that's a good question. I really don't remember. I think I was the first one in, so I don't remember closing it, but I think it was open when I pulled up to it."

"There's something else that seemed curious to me. I see multiple garages from this window. Do all of you have separate vehicles?"

"Oh, yes. Mine is the Lexus. Summer drives the pickup truck. The Jeep belongs to Spring. Autumn has a sports car, but she seldom drives it. And, of course, the Lamborghini is mother's. The old green Ford in the driveway there belongs to Mrs. Snook. We are well-supplied with vehicles."

"How about Giles? Does he have a car?"

"Actually, no. He has a friend who drives a taxi cab. Giles calls him when he needs to go somewhere."

"I see," Nash appeared to be deep in thought.

"Now, I have a question for you," Winter interrupted Nash's thoughts. "Do you think my sisters and I are in any danger?"

"I can't say for sure," Nash replied cautiously. "But I seriously doubt it. Your mother seems to have been the only target. If it turns out to be a murder attempt, it probably was directed only at her. But actually, Winter, the process has just begun. There's a lot yet to be discovered about the entire thing. I intend to keep searching for answers until this is solved.

"Here's my card just in case you think of anything." Nash finished.

"Please keep in touch," Winter said, extending her hand, her unusual blue eyes dancing with mischief. "I just might consider making you the private investigator in one of my novels."

"Personal investigator," Nash countered.

Winter's piercing blue eyes looked into his, and he felt suspended in time. Clearing his throat, he made a feeble attempt to assure her that he would indeed keep in touch and made his way downstairs and into the afternoon heat.

⟵——————————⟶

Nash wrestled with mixed feelings as he drove back to town and to the delicatessen where he picked up a picnic basket from Mr. Meijer.

"So, you and Katie having a picnic?" Mr. Meijer said in his broken English.

"Yes. We're going to the band concert in the park. It's been a long week, and I'm ready to relax a bit," Nash said pulling out his wallet and paying.

"Ah, good to relax. You work hard. Music is good for the soul," Mr. Meijer grinned, nodding his head. "I put some extra pickles in because I know how much Katie likes them."

"You are a kind man, Mr. Meijer," Nash assured him. "Thank you so much. I'd like to talk longer but need to get going."

Mr. Meijer nodded his head in understanding and shooed Nash on his way with his hands.

Nash hurried out the door realizing just how late he was going to be to pick up Katie. Thoughts of being with her filled his mind. Katie was just about the best thing in his life. She was considerate, understanding, and full of life. She knew just how to challenge him when necessary or how to make him laugh or when to sit quietly with him if the occasion called for it. Nash considered himself lucky.

He saw her waiting for him on the front steps of her house just as he turned the corner. His heart leaped as she waved. She looked ready for a summer evening in the park with her navy blue shorts and a red and white sleeveless top. Even though her brown eyes were covered by sunglasses, he knew they were filled with love for him.

"Hey," Nash said as he bounded up the steps of the porch.

He grabbed Katie and kissed her.

"Well, that's quite the greeting," she giggled. "One I like."

"Me, too," he admitted as he held her a little longer than usual. "It's been such a long, hot week. I just want to relax and enjoy the evening—with you!"

"That's just what I had in mind," Katie agreed as she picked up a small cooler from the porch floor.

The city park swelled with people whenever there was a band concert. Nash and Katie had just found a shady, unoccupied place to put their lawn chairs when the first strains of a rousing Sousa march filled the air. Nash stretched his legs out in front of him while Katie unwrapped the delicacies from the deli. The municipal band always played a great variety of music from classical to jazz to popular. There were waltzes and polkas and rock, as well. Nash relaxed from the cares of the day as he and Katie feasted on Mr. Meijer's picnic meal.

"The extra pickles are for you," Nash whispered. "Special from Mr. Meijer.

"He remembered," Katie smiled. "I must drop by to thank him."

Nash knew Katie would follow through on her promise. Her kindness was another quality he admired in her. As the evening progressed, Nash found Katie's hand and was overwhelmed by the comfort that afforded.

During the intermission, they left their seats to purchase ice cream cones from a local vender who always appeared on concert evenings with his ice cream cart. They walked slowly back to their seats, trying to keep the drips from reaching their hands and enjoying the slower pace of the evening.

"How's the case going?" Katie asked while licking the quickly melting ice cream. "Or do you not want to talk about it?"

"I don't mind talking about it. I haven't found any clues that I can really zero in on, yet. Anne is coming in to the office tomorrow morning, and we'll go over everything again together. I think my next step is hitting some of the resale shops. If someone has taken antique items, perhaps they have tried to sell them for cash."

"I'm off work for another few weeks. I could help with that if you want."

"I don't want to take advantage of your generosity, but that would be great. Meet me at the office about 9:00 tomorrow morning, and I'll give you pictures of the items. We also will make a list for you of the businesses that might have been involved."

"I'll be there."

# 9

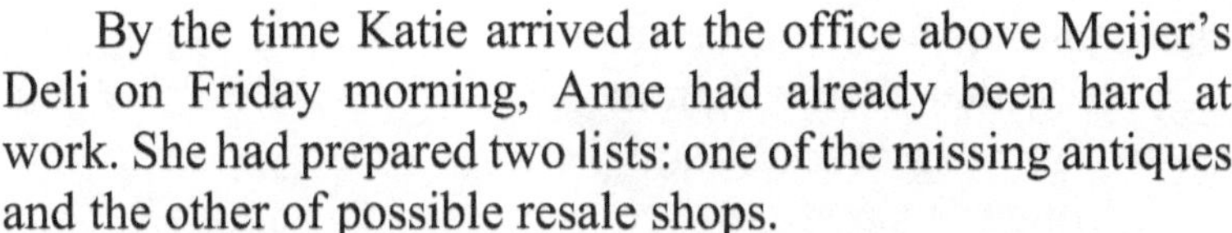

By the time Katie arrived at the office above Meijer's Deli on Friday morning, Anne had already been hard at work. She had prepared two lists: one of the missing antiques and the other of possible resale shops.

"You weren't kidding. Those are beautiful girls," Katie observed as she stepped through the office door and scanned the wall of information.

Nash nodded.

"But one of them could be a thief or an attempted murderer," he added.

"Which one would profit from stealing from her own family?"

"Actually, any of them—or none of them. They are given an allowance each month. I don't know the exact figures, but a couple of them have indicated it isn't a lot of money."

"Would they profit by killing their mother?"

"Maybe. Right now, they are bound by some mysterious clause in their father's will to remain in the home until the youngest turns twenty-five."

"And that is how many more years?"

"Five. Summer is the youngest, and she is twenty. But if you look at it from Winter's point of view, she will be in her thirties by then. And I'm quite sure she wants—as do all of them—to get on with her life.

"At least three of the girls have access to substances that could figure into possible poisoning—Summer with pesticides, Spring with drugs from the hospital, and Autumn with paint supplies. Winter is the only one who apparently doesn't have regular access to anything lethal."

Katie and Anne both nodded in agreement as Nash continued speaking.

"Anyway, Anne, Katie has volunteered to do some leg work at antique shops. Can you give her the things she needs to see if any of the stolen items have turned up. While she's doing that, I would like for you to dig deep and see what you can come up with on the lives of the Season family and include Walter Wainwright in your search. He may be able to shed some light on the situation."

"Walter Wainwright?"

"Yes. He's Holly's attorney."

"Where will you be, boss?" Anne asked.

"There are a couple of people I'd like to talk to that weren't on Holly's list," Nash said. "It's time I find out what Mrs. Snook and Giles might know. I'll meet you back here about 4:00, and then I'll take you both to supper at Clara's Café."

Giles met Nash at the door.

"Is madam expecting you?" he asked dryly.

"No. Actually, I'm not here to see Mrs. Season. I'd like to talk to you and Mrs. Snook."

Giles' eyebrows raised with quiet surprise, but he quickly resumed his usual lack of expression.

"Very good, sir," he replied. "Mrs. Season is napping. We can sit in the sun room if you like."

"That will be fine," Nash said and followed the small man to the room smothered with plants and the portrait of Mr. Season that hung over the fireplace.

"How can I be of help?" he asked as he sat timidly on the edge of one of the chairs.

"I just need a little more background," Nash began. "I take it that you've been with the Season family for quite some time—even while Mr. Season was alive."

Nash glanced at the portrait, and Giles seemed to relax a bit.

"Yes," Giles confirmed. "I was here before the birth of the four girls. I was here before Mr. and Mrs. Season were married. I've been with the family a very long time."

"You know, of course, about the missing items," Nash began.

"Yes—the Royal Doulton China, a set of eight Waterford crystal wine glasses, the Nippon hand-painted tea pot, the Wedgwood sage green footed bowl, the Wedgwood blue candle holders, and the Tiffany lamp. It was such a shame. They had been in the family for generations."

Nash noted that Giles seemed to be well-informed on the missing items.

"I'm not an expert on antiques, but I'm guessing those items are very rare and expensive."

"Oh, yes, sir. They would bring a fair price these days."

"Do you have any idea as to who would take those?"

"Not really. Well…" Giles hesitated.

"Is there something more?" Nash quizzed.

"No. No, there couldn't be. It's just that Miss Winter has been acting strangely since this whole thing was discovered. You know, the items were taken shortly after her return from her trip to Africa. I've always wondered if there was a connection. That had to be an expensive trip. But, no, I'm quite sure she would be incapable of doing such a thing."

Nash studied the elderly man's face for a time before he spoke.

"Any thoughts on the possible poisoning?"

"No. None. Has any more been discovered about that?"

"Not yet."

Giles nodded his head as if he understood. Then Holly, who had apparently awakened from her nap, summoned him by demanding her cup of tea.

"If you'll excuse me," Giles said, responding quickly to the call.

"Of course. If you think of anything else, please feel free to call me," Nash said, slipping him a card.

Giles hurried from the sun room while Nash made his way to the kitchen. Mrs. Snook was busy peeling vegetables at the kitchen sink for the evening meal. She startled when she saw Nash.

"Oh, Lord, have mercy! I knew you'd be askin' some questions of me," she nervously defended herself as she retrieved her dropped paring knife. "I swear I had nothin' to do with Mrs. Season or her unfortunate accident."

"Mmm. I love the aroma of a kitchen," Nash declared in an effort to calm the middle-aged cook's heightened anxiety.

"Are you just here to check out my cooking?" she asked suspiciously.

"No, I just want to ask you a few questions," Nash began.

"Oh, Lord, have mercy! I'm a good cook. I'm a good person," she wailed as she wiped her hands on her apron and turned towards him. "Ain't nothin' like this ever happened before to anyone I've fed. I would never do anything to hurt anyone."

"No one is accusing you of anything," Nash soothed. "It's just that you may have some piece of information that could shed some light on the situation. I find that sometimes people know more than they realize. And any little bit of information can be helpful. Come sit down and rest a minute."

Nash gestured toward one of the chairs at the kitchen table, and Mrs. Snook begrudgingly obliged. She began to sniffle as she edged her pudgy body into the chair. Nash sat across from her while she wiped her eyes and then blew her nose.

"Something smells really good," Nash said, attempting to calm the woman again.

"Pot roast," she managed before she once again became emotional. "I swear I don't know nothin' about any of this. My reputation will be ruined if any of this gets out—I can't believe that it was my food that poisoned poor Ms. Season. Oh, Lord, have mercy!"

"Please, calm yourself. I enjoyed the dinner I ate. And remember, none of the rest of us got sick. Don't worry. We'll find out how this happened and clear your name."

"Lord, have mercy! I hope so!"

"Please, answer some questions for me so I can help you," Nash asked, waiting until she blotted her eyes again and nodded her head in agreement before continuing. "You are here throughout the entire day? Every day?"

"Yes, sir. I get here about 5:00 in the morning, and I leave about 8:00 or 9:00 at night. Ms. Season sometimes lets me sleep over if I want. There's a cot in the small room just off the kitchen. She's always been nice to me. I would never do anything to hurt her," she reiterated.

With that, Mrs. Snook began to bawl again. She wiped her eyes on the tail of her apron, and Nash waited until she was calmer before continuing.

"Do you recall any strangers being in the house last Friday? Like a delivery person or someone who is not normally here?"

"No. No one. Any deliveries are made at the door. No one enters the house. There's just been Ms. Season and the girls."

"And Giles? Does he spend much time in the kitchen?"

"Some. He helps me some. And he helps serve the meals. But I can't imagine—"

"I imagine," Nash interrupted her before her mind could wander again, "since you've been here quite a few years, that you've taught the girls a few things about cooking. Do they like to cook?"

"Well, not Miss Autumn or Miss Spring. They are seldom in the kitchen except to get food that's already prepared. But Miss Summer, now, she likes to bake, especially cookies. But she don't do that much in the summertime 'cause she's busy and all outside. What she likes is to bake for the winter holidays. Now, Miss Winter, well, she could be a right nice cook if she wanted to be. She likes to cook, and she's good at it, too. She doesn't always have time with her busy schedule, but when she's not on assignment, she spends a lot of time in the kitchen dreamin' up concoctions just like she dreams up those books."

"You know about the missing antique items, right?"

"Oh, yes. What a terrible thing! I was the one who found the cabinet doors open and the things gone. The police came and dusted for fingerprints, but they didn't find anything other than those that belong to the family, and of course, Giles and me."

"Mrs. Snook, I'm going to give you one of my cards. My phone number is on it. Feel free to call me any time you might think of something that could be helpful. By the way, that pot roast really does smell good."

A smile spread over Mrs. Snook's face. "That be the pot roast all right," she said as she stood. "I was just ready to put the vegetables in it when you came in."

"My mom's a pretty good cook, too, and I can tell that pot roast is going to make for one amazing dinner."

Mrs. Snook was all smiles. "And apple pie for dessert," she beamed.

"If you tell me any more about the delicacies you are preparing, I might be tempted to beg for an invitation," Nash smiled and winked.

"Lord, have mercy!" Mrs. Snook declared as a broad smile spread across her face. "I'd like feedin' such a nice young man with an appetite for good food."

"One more question. Is Mrs. Season difficult to please?"

There was a pause.

"She didn't used to be. Seems like things have changed as the years has gone by. But then I guess they have for all of us. Lord, have mercy! I'm not as young as I used to be."

"But you're still a great cook," Nash winked.

"Go on with you," Mrs. Snook blushed.

Armed with photos of the missing items from the Season's house and the list of likely antique shops, Katie set out to see what she could find. Her cell phone also contained photos of the four daughters. Although each shop owner was different—some skeptical, some secretive—it seemed as if they all had the same response. No, they had not seen the merchandise or the girls. She was told over and over again that if any of the four girls had been in the store, they would have been unforgettable.

Some shops were filled with nothing more than junk. Others were upscale. Katie had looked at more old glassware and antiques than she ever thought possible. She stopped her car in front of a rather small shop. Printed in cursive lettering on the window were the words, "Bits and Pieces." Taking a long drink of cool water from her thermos, she opened the car door. Moving from the air-conditioned car into the intense heat was grueling. She hurried through the shop door where a young woman greeted her.

"My name is Katie, and I'm looking for some information for personal investigator, Nash Adams. He is working on a case involving some stolen antiques. I wonder if I might show you some photos of the missing items."

"I guess that would be all right," the woman seemed hesitant.

Katie held out the papers containing the missing items and their descriptions. The young woman studied them carefully and then shook her head.

"I'm sorry. I don't recognize any of these items," she said. "They are quite valuable, and I'm sure anyone in this shop would have questioned anyone trying to sell them."

"How about any of these women?" Katie said as she brought the photos up on her cell phone.

Once again, the woman studied the photos and shook her head.

"Wait! Oh, this one!" she exclaimed. "The blonde with the short hair. She was in here a few days ago."

"Did she have items to sell?"

"Yes. Yes, as a matter of fact, she *was* selling something. But it wasn't any of those things you showed me. It was a ring, a rather unique ring. I'm sure we still have it. Many people have looked at it, but no one has made an offer. I believe it's…yes, here it is!"

The woman produced a small glass case that contained several rings. She pointed to the one in question. Its beauty took Katie's breath away. A pink rose painted on porcelain placed in a gold setting. It truly was striking.

"Would it be all right if I took a photo of this?" she asked.

"Let me check," the woman said and went to the back room, returning shortly, having obtained permission.

"Thank you," Katie said as she snapped the photo. "Here is Nash Adams' card. If any of these items appear in your shop, we'd appreciate it if you could give him a call."

Once again in the cool of her car, Katie headed for the last establishment on her list: Mr. Alex's Antiques. As she entered the building and sank into the deep carpet, she thought this was the most elegant of all the shops she had entered that day. Items were tastefully displayed and soft music played in the background. Mr. Alex himself, dressed in suit and tie, greeted her.

"How can I be of help?" he asked softly.

Katie explained her mission as she had at all the other shops throughout the day. She was suddenly conscious of her now wrinkled clothing and the way perspiration lingered on her face and hair. She followed Mr. Alex to his air-conditioned office and was more than pleased when he offered her a seat and some cold water. She sat quietly while he perused the papers with the missing items.

"No. None of these items have come through our shop," he finally said as he pushed the papers back across his desk.

"How about any of these young women?" she sighed, disappointed by his response. "Have you seen any of them?"

"Oh, yes," he said. "This one was here just a few days ago."

"Can you tell me if she was selling anything?"

"No, she was not. As a matter of fact, I believe she was asking about these same items."

Katie thanked Mr. Alex, gave him one of Nash's cards, and left the spaciousness of Mr. Alex's Antiques.

By 3:30 in the afternoon, a tired and discouraged Katie was driving back to the office to meet up with Anne and Nash.

Anne stood from her place at her desk and stretched her arms above her head to relieve the tension in her body. She had been in front of the computer ever since Nash and Katie had left the office. As well as hitting dozens of websites on the computer, she had also made several telephone calls. Efficient as she was, it was no surprise there was a sizeable stack of notes on her desk. She glanced at the clock: 4:00. She anticipated that both Nash and Katie would soon arrive and the three of them could share their findings. She did not have to wait long. Nash was the first to return.

"Productive day?" Anne asked.

"You know what I always say: another piece of the puzzle," Nash replied.

Anne watched with interest as Nash began adding to the wall of pertinent information. Before long, photos of Giles and Mrs. Snook were posted, and information was written underneath their pictures. A tired Katie soon joined the co-workers. Three exhausted people aimed their chairs toward the wall. With bottles of cold water in their hands, they began to quietly analyze the information before them. Nash allowed a few minutes of reflection before he spoke.

"Where you able to find anything, Katie?" he asked.

"Not much," she sighed. "I went to every place on this list but only came up with two little bits of information. It seems as though Summer Season was at Bits & Pieces. Winter was at Mr. Alex's Antiques. Neither establishment had seen any of the missing items, however."

"Were you able to find out what the girls were doing there? Were they buying or selling?" Nash inquired.

"Summer sold some jewelry, a ring to be specific. Was there a ring reported as missing?"

"I haven't seen a missing ring on any list," Anne interjected.

"Then I don't know where it came from. Here's a picture of it."

Katie passed her cell phone around so both Anne and Nash could see the item.

"What about Winter? You said she had been to Alex's Antiques?" Nash asked once he had examined image of the ring.

"Yes. Mr. Alex was very cooperative and seemed concerned," Anne explained. "It appears that Winter had been there and was inquiring about the missing pieces as well. Perhaps doing a little sleuthing on her own?"

"That doesn't surprise me. It sounds like Winter," Nash observed as he added Katie's findings to the wall.

When he finished, Anne was ready to move on. "How about you?" she asked. "Were either Giles or Mrs. Snook helpful?"

"Giles seems well informed about things happening in the house—maybe a little too well-informed. He shed a little suspicion in Winter's direction, and I'm still trying to decide if there was anything behind that. Mrs. Snook was a nervous wreck as I expected her to be. I'm convinced she had nothing to do with any of this. She did, however, tell me that two of the girls—Summer and Winter—are familiar with the kitchen."

"Seems as though Winter's name is coming up frequently. Should that put more suspicion on her?" Katie asked.

"It could. I'm just not sure yet. How about you, Anne? Did you find out anything?" Nash asked.

"Yes, I did. The allowance the girls receive is really a very small amount. If they weren't living at the mansion, I don't think they could make it on their own except for Spring. She makes enough as a nurse to be independent. But the financials for the other women seem to be pretty meager.

That may tie into Katie's information about Summer selling some jewelry."

Katie and Nash waited while the efficient Anne systematically worked her way through each page of her notes.

"Some of this may be repetitious. Mrs. Snook has been in the Season employ for about ten years now. She lives alone but has one daughter who lives in Boston with a granddaughter. She visits them once a year. Other than that, she seems content to cook and clean for the Season family.

"Giles was with Mr. Season's parents before Stormy married Holiday. There's not much on him. He just seems to be a permanent fixture at the estate. No bank account, no credit card activity.

"Summer was an excellent student in high school and graduated at the top of her class but refused to attend the graduation ceremonies. Despite being a good student, she was frequently in trouble for numerous pranks and unconventional behavior. Last year she was approached by some gardening magazine that wanted to do an article on her gardens at Season manor, but she refused. I couldn't find a reason. Summer is well-known at some of the upscale night clubs in the area, but, like Cinderella, it seems she exits just as the party gets started.

"Spring has been in her present position for almost two years. She is well-thought of by her co-workers, especially one young man—a Titus McNerny who works in medical imaging. She had an offer from a well-known Chicago hospital but turned it down.

"Winter was captain of her swim team in high school. She is the only one who was sent away during her high school years to attend private school. She freelances and has had articles in several magazines. As you already discovered, she recently returned from a trip to Africa. She has had several relationships with young men, but they never seem to last very long.

"I couldn't find much on Autumn. Her interest in art started at an early age. She pretty much keeps to herself. I did find something interesting though. It seems that her mother, Holly, also had an interest in art while she was in college. That brings us to Holiday.

"Holiday Carter met Frederick Season while they were in college out East. Her family was not wealthy like the Seasons were. She did not finish college but dropped out to marry Frederick. Winter was born 8 months later.

"Frederick Season was voted by his fraternity brothers to be most likely to make his first million dollars by age twenty-five. College is where he got his nickname, 'Stormy.' He seems to have had an interest in sailing." She paused. "You do see the humor in that, right? Stormy Season…sailing? Well, anyway, he played football in college and lived what some people refer to as the good life.

"I really had to dig and go through some back doors, but I finally was able to look at a copy of Mr. Season's will. It does indeed state that the girls are to remain in the household until the youngest is twenty-five under penalty of receiving nothing from the estate.

"Now, about Mr. Wainwright—I didn't find out much. He seems to be a reputable lawyer and has been handling legal matters for the Season family for quite a few years. I did, however, find out that he and Mr. Season were fraternity brothers in college. It appears they were very close and even stood up to witness each other's weddings. He married Marjorie Sacks about the same time Holiday and Frederick were married. The Wainwright marriage didn't last, however. But there is something interesting I dug up. Marjorie Sacks Wainwright is now Marjorie Fortune—yes, the same woman who is on the city council. I would suggest that might be worth looking in to."

That was Anne—always thinking ahead and planning. She continued.

"Then I went to the financials. Nash, the Season family is not what it appears to be. They are basically broke—or close to it. It started before Mr. Season died three years ago and has continued to decline ever since."

"Wow!" Nash commented. "Good work. Where once we had a sketch, we are beginning to fill in the entire picture. Just out of curiosity, see if you can set up a meeting with Marjorie Fortune. It might be interesting to see what she has to say."

Once the tired trio finished comparing notes, they were more than happy to put away the stress of the day and grab a bite to eat. Anne jumped in Katie's car, and Nash drove separately to Clara's Café. Nash liked to support local businesses when he could. Clara herself met them at their table with her jovial smile.

"It's a hot one out there today," she said, wiping her hands on her white apron. "It's the first thing talked about in here all day long. It's been good for business, though. Nobody wants to spend today in a hot kitchen."

"So, business is good?" Nash smiled back at the matronly lady.

"All day today. The breakfast crowd spilled over into the lunch bunch."

"Well, I hope you have some food left for three starving people," he joked.

"Depends on what you want," she replied. "But I do have a piece of that lemon pie you like so much."

"Sold," Nash agreed. "Plus, three hamburger platters, if you please."

"Comin' right up," the owner, waitress, and cook beamed.

It did not take long for three frosty soft drinks to be delivered to their table. They discussed their theories about the information they had gathered in low tones. Clara delivered the platters of food to their table in a timely fashion and then moved on to serve others entering the small diner.

"There's one thing that still puzzles me," Anne mentioned as she dipped another French fry in ketchup. "Why do four apparently modern young women remain in such a stifling situation? This isn't 1920. I would think they would have rebelled a long time ago."

"I think it's probably loyalty to their deceased father," Katie offered. "I sense the girls were close to their dad."

"Hey, I thought we weren't going to discuss work?" Nash teased. "But, I think Katie may be correct in her assessment. The tie to their father seems to be a strong one. And perhaps it's just a more comfortable place for them to be."

Just then, lightning streaked across the sky, and the trio heard thunder in the distance.

"Looks like we're going to get that storm they've been promising," Anne observed as she peered out the window at the darkening sky.

"Anything to relieve this heat and humidity," Katie replied.

"Maybe it's Stormy Season trying to send us a message," Nash chimed in. His remark was met with a roll of Anne's eyes. "All right. So maybe it wasn't such a great joke."

"I think living in the same house with Tony has caused his personality to rub off on you," Katie teased.

The impending storm soon became the focus of all the customers in Clara's Café. Even Clara stood in the doorway looking out at the tumbling storm clouds while gusts of wind began to blow debris along the street. Several customers hurried through their meals, hoping to get to their vehicles before the storm broke. It had been such a long, hot week. The length of the heat wave had sapped everyone's energy. Nash, Katie, and Anne were content to relax and enjoy the hamburgers.

A louder crash of thunder coming at the same time his cell phone rang caused Nash to startle.

"Hello," he answered. "Slow down…Just what is going on?"

Anne and Katie grew quiet as they listened to the urgency in Nash's voice and watched the concern spread over his face.

"Yes…Yes, I'll be there as soon as I can."

"What's going on? Bad news?" Katie asked as Nash sat staring at his phone.

"That was Winter Season. Holly is at the hospital—again. Same symptoms. You girls can stay here if you want. I'm going to run by there to see what I can find out."

"Do what you have to do," Katie told him as she put her hand on his. "And watch out for the storm," she added.

Nash nodded and rushed from the restaurant into the blustery wind. He glanced up at the sky swirling ominously above. Not wasting any more time, Nash hurried toward his old Chevy.

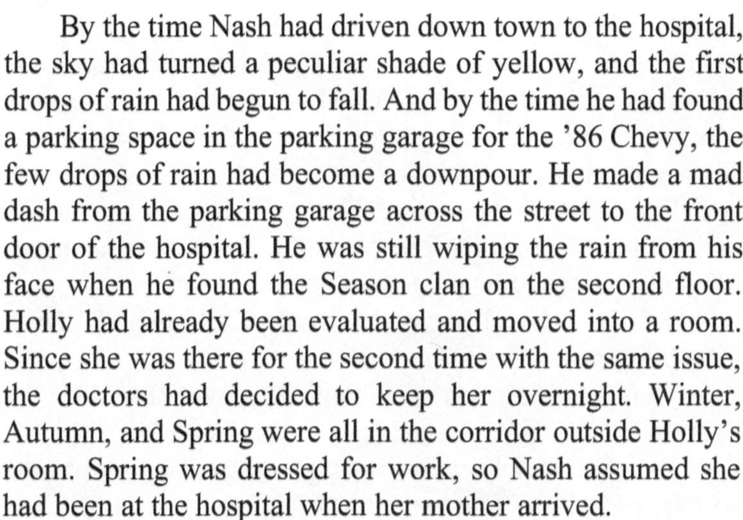

## 10

By the time Nash had driven down town to the hospital, the sky had turned a peculiar shade of yellow, and the first drops of rain had begun to fall. And by the time he had found a parking space in the parking garage for the '86 Chevy, the few drops of rain had become a downpour. He made a mad dash from the parking garage across the street to the front door of the hospital. He was still wiping the rain from his face when he found the Season clan on the second floor. Holly had already been evaluated and moved into a room. Since she was there for the second time with the same issue, the doctors had decided to keep her overnight. Winter, Autumn, and Spring were all in the corridor outside Holly's room. Spring was dressed for work, so Nash assumed she had been at the hospital when her mother arrived.

"Thanks for coming, Nash," Winter said as she approached him, her steely blue eyes showing gratitude as well as concern.

"What's going on?" he asked. "Have they told you anything yet?"

"Only that the symptoms are the same as before. They pumped her stomach and have given her something for the pain and nausea. She's resting now."

"I'm sure you've gone over all the possibilities," Nash continued. "Perhaps if we go over them again, something will pop up that we overlooked. Has she eaten anything different? Have there been any strangers in the house?"

The answer was no to both questions. Nothing out of the ordinary had gone on at the Season mansion. The discussion was interrupted by a flurry of activity behind them as Summer made her entrance.

"Now what?" she asked as she joined her sisters.

"The same as before," Spring explained. "Winter and Autumn brought her in right away, and she's getting the best treatment."

"Why is this happening?" Summer was distraught.

"We don't know," Winter added. "But they are going to keep her overnight to run some more tests."

As soon as she noticed Nash, she burst into tears and rushed into his arms. He felt awkward as he tried to both soothe her and keep her at a distance. After a few seconds, she stepped back and sniffled.

"Enough with the drama," Spring frowned at her sister's antics. "I need to get back to work. Dr. Edwards is in charge of Mother's case. She is in good hands."

"Would it be all right if I went in to see her?" Nash asked.

"Sure. She's alert and probably would enjoy the distraction."

Just then Giles came huffing and puffing down the hallway. He was drenched and was carrying a bag. It was obviously quite a walk for the elderly man.

"How is she?" he asked as he sat the bag down and proceeded to mop his head.

"Resting." Nash heard Autumn's answer before ducking into the room.

Holly was sitting up in bed when Nash entered the room. Although she appeared to be tired, she still maintained her aura of being in control. Her face lit up when she saw him.

"I didn't expect you to come," she said and then added, "But I'm glad you did."

"Well, I thought I'd just check things out," he explained. "We need to find out what is going on with you. Have the doctors told you anything?"

"Just that it appears to be some kind of poisoning. Before you start grilling me, I know all your questions, and the answers are still the same as last time. I've not had anything suspicious to eat, and there has been no one new in the house. Honestly, Nash, there are no clues."

"Finding out what poison it is will give us a clue, but that may take some time. The local lab here at the hospital is still working on it and samples have been sent to the state. You know how that works. It all takes time. Labs are busy and technicians overworked. This is going to require some patience."

"Something I'm sure you are aware that I am lacking," she smiled as she extended her hand toward him. "I really appreciate your coming."

"I'll be in touch," Nash encouraged. "Giles is here with some things you requested, so he will probably be in to see you next. Then you need to get some rest."

Holly nodded in agreement and lay her head back on the pillow as Nash returned to the hallway. Giles seemed eager to get into the room to finish delivering the items Holly had requested. Nash knew there was nothing more he could do here, and he needed to be on his way home. Spring had gone back to work, but the other three girls were huddled together in discussion. Assuring them that he would keep in touch, he headed down to the hospital entrance. As he stepped out into the storm, he saw Walter Wainwright on his way inside.

Nash sloshed through a puddle, which got his feet wet and added to his discomfort. The parking garage had a certain dankness about it. He saw Summer's blue pickup truck parked in a spot near his Chevy. He was preoccupied with thoughts of getting home and out of the weather when he saw it. His passenger side rear tire was flat. In spite of being exhausted from the heat and uncomfortable from the rain, he opened the trunk of the car, pulled out the jack and spare tire, loosened the lug nuts, and started jacking up the car.

Once the spare was on, he reversed the process and surveyed his work. It looked as if the spare would hold until he could get home. Throwing the damaged tire and the tools back into the trunk, he slid behind the wheel. He was more than ready to find a hot shower and get some rest.

He frowned. Taped to the steering wheel was a piece of paper. On it was scribbled the following words: "Quit snooping or something worse might happen."

He looked around at the other vehicles nearby. All was quiet. Surely no one would have stayed around after placing the note on the steering wheel anyway. He saw nothing out of the ordinary in the dark. After rummaging for some plastic bags he kept handy for evidence, he carefully placed the note in one of them. He hoped Louie could get some fingerprints from it.

All the way home Nash went over the note in his head. Apparently, someone did not appreciate him asking questions and snooping around, but Nash had more questions that needed answers.

Typically, Saturday mornings were filled with projects around the house. Nash rubbed his hand over his unruly hair as he made his way to the breakfast table.

"Where's Tony?" he yawned as he pulled out a chair.

"He went in to work at the garage," Ma told him. "Overtime. There were lots of cars that couldn't get finished through the week."

Nash nodded as Ma placed a plate of scrambled eggs and toast in front of him.

"What about you?" Ma asked. "You got plans for today?"

"Sort of," Nash said cautiously. "Do you have something you need done?"

"No. No, I'm doing some baking for Sunday dinner. Nothing special."

"I thought I'd go down and talk with Louie a bit."

"Something break in the case?"

"Not really, Ma," Nash evaded the question. "Just a development. And I think I'll stop by the garage and see Tony as well. I had a flat tire last night so I need to get that taken care of."

"Umm-hmm," Ma nodded as she sifted flour into a large bowl.

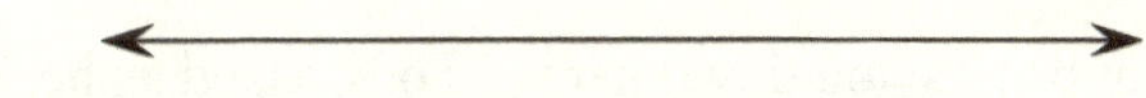

"Glad you're in the office this morning," Nash said to Louie as he approached the always busy desk.

"Make it quick," Louie answered as he looked up from his paperwork. "I don't intend to be here much longer."

"I won't keep you," Nash said as he laid the plastic bag with the ominous note on Louie's desk.

"What's this?" Louie asked as he picked up the bag and read the note. "You being threatened?"

"Looks like it. I just wanted to know if you could run it for fingerprints."

"Sure. Don't know if Chafee is in today, but I'll get it to him and let you know when I know something. How did this come about?"

"I was at the hospital because Holly had another incident. Parked in the parking garage across the street.

When I came back out of the hospital, I found a flat tire and this was on the steering wheel."

"You think the two are connected?"

"Don't know. I didn't think about it at the time."

"Hmm," Louie nodded. "Be careful, Nash. You must be getting close enough to bother somebody."

"Will do. See you tomorrow for Sunday dinner?"

"I'll be there."

Nash's second stop of the morning was Clyde's garage where he found his little brother under the hood of a Ford truck.

"What brings you down here?" Tony asked as he wiped his hands and slammed the hood of the truck shut.

"I had a flat last night. Thought I'd better see if it can be repaired or if I need a new one. It's in the trunk."

Tony lifted the trunk lid and pulled out the damaged tire to examine it.

"How'd you say this happened?" he quizzed.

"I was in the parking garage by the hospital. When I came back to the car, I found the tire was flat."

"Guess you didn't look at it very carefully," Tony observed.

"Nope. I was wet and tired. I just changed it and threw it in the trunk. Why?"

"Look here," Tony said as he pointed to the damage. "This just didn't go down because it had a slow leak or something. Someone has deliberately punctured it. Look at these holes. Looks like maybe a screwdriver or an awl or an ice pick or something like that. And not just one stab, but several."

A chill ran through Nash's body as he saw exactly what Tony had observed.

"Wow!"

"I guess, '*wow!*' It certainly had to be intentional. What have you gotten yourself into, big brother? Does this have anything to do with the Season case?"

"Right now, I don't have the answers," Nash replied. "It could be, but I don't know anything for sure. Could be some random vandalism. At any rate, let's just not mention this to Ma. Wouldn't want her to worry."

Nash could tell Tony did not buy the statement about random vandalism but at least he did not pressure him further for answers.

All the way to his appointment with Marjorie Fortune, Nash went over the facts from the previous evening in his head. The car had been all right when he arrived at the hospital. He would have known if he were driving on a flat. No, he was quite sure the tire was intact when he parked the car in the parking garage. He also had not seen anything unusual in the surrounding area.

His mind went to the obvious suspects. When he arrived, Winter, Spring, and Autumn were all in the hallway outside Holiday's room. He was sure none of them left the area while he was there. That pretty much eliminated them. Then he remembered. It was Summer who came late, and it was Summer's blue pickup he had seen parked several spaces over from where he had parked. Was Summer the culprit? What was it Tony had said? A screwdriver, ice pick, or an awl? Probably all of those could be found in Summer's tool box. Nash's stomach began to churn at the possibility.

⟵—————————————⟶

Anne had been swift in setting up the appointment with Marjorie Fortune. Nash waited for the councilwoman near the courts of the local tennis club. From his seat at one of the glass-topped tables, he had a clear view of players coming in from the courts. Although he had never formally met Councilwoman Fortune, he had seen her multiple times when he and Louie were working on Ella's Place. He absently swished the ice in his glass of Pepsi.

After fifteen more minutes, he glanced impatiently at his watch as a group of players walked toward him. One of them, a tall and very tan woman, broke off from the group when she spied Nash. He got to his feet to greet her, relieved his wait had ended.

Marjorie Fortune was one of those women who could be intimidating just by her presence. It was a quality that made her a force on the city council. She wore a white tennis outfit that highlighted her deep tan. Her hair was pulled back into a ponytail with a pink scrunchie that matched her pink socks. Her entire outfit gave her the appearance of youth. Tiny beads of perspiration dotted her forehead. Her pale blue eyes did not miss anything about the young investigator. Her look was unnerving. She grasped his hand with a very firm handshake.

"You must be Nash Adams," she said as she gestured for him to resume sitting. "I'm Marjorie."

"It's a pleasure meeting you," Nash replied, struggling with how to address her. He decided to let his remark stand alone. "Thank you for meeting with me."

She ignored his pleasantries and looked at him with her piercing blue eyes.

"Just what can I help you with?" she was all about the business at hand. "Is there a problem with your renovation project?"

"Oh, no. That's going well. I'm here because I am working on a case with the Season family, and I understand your former husband is the attorney for them. It's been brought to my attention that you and your husband were good friends with the Seasons at one time. I was just wondering if you were comfortable sharing any information about that time that might be of help to my case."

The answer to his question was obvious. Marjorie Fortune frowned and became uncomfortable.

"I don't know what I could possible share…" she began and then paused. "I haven't seen Holiday for a very long time. That was all a long time ago. Walter and I have been divorced for many years."

"I understand," Nash continued. "I don't want to dredge up bad memories, but I thought some insight on those early years might help."

"Just what is it you want to know?"

"Anything at all about the college days or the early days of their marriage that might impact the stability of their family today."

Marjorie's face turned dark. It was as if she became an entirely different person from the poised and in-command woman who had first sat across the table from him. She reached for her tennis racket, and Nash thought she was going to leave.

"Please," he murmured.

Marjorie relaxed and put the tennis racket back in its place. She leaned forward and looked directly into Nash's eyes.

"I repeat, Mr. Adams. I do not understand what I could possibly tell you that would help you."

Nash continued to sit quietly. Finally, Marjorie sank back in her chair and sighed.

"We were all young—very young," she finally began. "Stormy and Walter were roommates at the fraternity. My father was well-to-do, but nothing compared to the wealth of the Season family. Walter and Holiday had to work very hard to afford college tuition, but Walter was very serious about his career. Stormy wasn't what you would call a dedicated student. He was always about having a good time even if it might have been at someone else's expense. He had the good times and then used Walter to pull him out of a lot of situations."

"Situations?"

"All kinds of things—covering up pranks, drinking, partying, gambling, girls. Stormy was in it to enjoy college, and Walter was always there to pick up the pieces for him, so to speak. I guess that gave him good experience for his future career."

"And Holiday?"

Marjorie frowned as she looked off in the distance, obviously remembering with pain.

"We were friends—once. Holly came from a very poor family. Her biggest asset was her beauty, but she was a talented artist. Stormy was immediately taken with her, and she was thrilled to be included in a world she'd never known before. They became inseparable, that is, until she got pregnant. Then, once again, Stormy turned to Walter to get him out of the mess he'd gotten himself into. He wanted Walter to convince Holly to have an abortion and set up the appointment—keeping Stormy's name out of it."

She paused, and Nash waited a moment before he spoke.

"Walter couldn't—wouldn't?"

"It just so happened that Stormy wasn't the only one who was in love with Holly. Walter was in love with her, too." Marjorie said bitterly. "I'm quite sure he would have married her and raised the child as his own, but a part of him wanted Stormy to take responsibility for his actions—to hold him accountable. Plus, Holly was so into Stormy, she wouldn't look at another guy even after Stormy suggested the abortion."

Nash waited while Marjorie brushed aside a tear that slid down her cheek.

"Finally, Walter threatened to tell Stormy's parents about his gambling problem if he didn't do right by Holly. That seemed to work. Stormy and Holly got married. Holly dropped out of school. And Stormy kept right on being the playboy. And a few months later, Walter and I were married. End of story."

"But Walter got his law degree and became the Seasons' lawyer."

"Yes. He's always kept in touch with her. I've come to believe it was because he still cared for her and wanted to protect her."

Nash noted that Marjorie only extended Walter's desire to protect to Holly and not Stormy. He stared at the brave, yet vulnerable woman sitting across from him. He saw a side of Marjorie Fortune that probably no one else knew. She had moved on from the past and created a life for herself, far from the expectations of the innocent co-ed she had been.

"This is something I don't normally talk about, Mr. Adams. I hope you will be discreet with the information I've shared with you."

"Of course," Nash said, meekly. "I understand how personal this is for you and how much courage it took to reveal it."

Marjorie nodded and reached for her tennis racket. Nash watched her as she walked away almost wishing he had not pressured her for the information. At the same time, what she revealed explained a few things about this case and perhaps sent it in another direction.

## 11

"I can't eat another bite," Louie groaned as he pushed his dessert plate from in front of him. "I think I have sinned on this day."

"At least, if we have to take you to the hospital, we'll know the cause," Tony explained. "It will be over-indulgence, not Ma's cooking."

"It's my own lack of discipline," Louie admitted as he grinned at Ma. "I take full responsibility. I have to admit that I anticipate this day all week long."

"You should eat better," Ma advised in her kind, motherly way.

"What? And ruin the expectation of Sunday dinner at the Adams' table?"

"Nash, there's an article in this morning's newspaper that might interest you," Midge interjected as she left the table and then returned with the paper for her brother.

"Where?" Nash asked as he took the newspaper from her.

"Page 3. It seems as if someone you know is participating in a lecture at the library tomorrow evening. It might be of interest to you."

Nash found the page and scanned the article. He read aloud: "Journalist Winter Season will join Professor Harlin Scutter in a lecture on their recent trip to Africa. 7:30 p.m. at the downtown library branch, room 17. The public is invited."

"I might be able to find another clue at this lecture," he mused. "Anybody care to attend?"

Immediately, Anne and Katie volunteered.

"I'd like to go, but I have a genealogy meeting," Midge said blushing. All present knew she had met her guy friend, Clark, at the meetings.

"Uh, a lecture on Africa doesn't sound like my thing," Louie declined.

"Don't look at me," Tony added. "Sounds b-o-r-i-n-g at best."

"Okay, I'll pick up you gals tomorrow then, and we'll see what Winter and the professor have to say." Then, Nash turned to Louie and asked, "Hey, are we on for a run in the morning?"

Louie groaned and patted his stomach.

"You may have to push me in a wheelbarrow," he laughed.

"There's more of a crowd than I expected," Nash observed as they pulled into the library parking lot. "For now, let's just pretend we don't know each other. We can sit apart. It may not be important, but we may be able to gather more information that way."

Katie took a seat up front near the podium. Anne sat over to the left of the main aisle, and Nash settled in near the back row on the right. Professor Scutter was a tall middle-aged man with a splattering of gray in his dark unkempt hair. He was slender, wore glasses, and Nash thought he fit the perfect description of a professor. He fumbled with the sheaf of papers in his hand so much that Nash feared he would drop them all over the platform.

Winter made her entrance amid hushed comments from the audience. She was dressed in khaki shorts and shirt, hiking boots, and a white pith helmet one typically expects to see on a safari. Nash mused that she sure knew how to make an entrance. A table displayed several artifacts that Nash assumed were to be used in the presentation.

Professor Scutter was the first to speak after formal introductions were made. It was fifteen minutes of painfully boring material. Nash thought perhaps Tony was correct in his earlier assessment of the evening. However, Winter's turn at the microphone was like a breath of fresh air. She was bubbly, exciting, and funny. While Professor Scutter dwelt on scientific facts and statistics, Winter added details about the human-interest part of the trip. She told of the people they had met and how they lived and survived. She discussed at length the native diet and how foods were hunted and prepared. She told of the tasks each member of the family was expected to perform. Even though thousands of miles from its more civilized counterparts, the political structure of the village had evolved.

When it came to medical details, Professor Scutter once again resumed the dialogue. He explained how natives used herbs and plants as medicinal cures, and Nash found himself actually interested. Winter's contribution had apparently spurred the professor to be more down to earth in his presentation. Nash's thoughts drifted as he pictured himself on safari in the wilds of Africa, experiencing some of the things he was hearing. He was surprised when the applause from the audience woke him from his daydream.

He stood at the back of the room at the conclusion of the presentation while he watched Katie engage Winter in conversation. He was pleasantly surprised when he saw the timid Anne approach Professor Scutter. He was quite sure Professor Scutter was being asked the most thought-provoking questions.

Nash was drawn to the table of artifacts and found them quite fascinating . There were utensils for preparing food. There were leaves, berries, nuts, and barks that were used in poultices and syrups. Some simple tools used for planting were on display, as well. He waited until he saw Katie yield to the line of people who waited to speak with Winter before joining the line himself. Surprisingly, when Winter saw him, she by-passed those who were ahead of him and went directly to him.

"Nash," she smiled as she grasped his hand, "I'm pleasantly surprised to see you here. I didn't know you were interested in Africa."

"Well, maybe not so much the presentation as the presenter," he charmed.

"Isn't Professor Scutter fabulous?" she gushed, graciously skirting his compliment. "That man is such a wealth of knowledge."

"You weren't so bad yourself."

"Well, I do the best I can, but I don't have all those facts and figures."

Nash thought she did well in that department without comment.

The following morning, Nash and Anne sat in the upstairs office catching up on paperwork. As usual, efficient Anne had her planner and pencil in hand.

"Mrs. Wagner is coming in today," Anne told him as she handed him a manila envelope. "We have the information she requested about her husband's whereabouts on Wednesday afternoons. Everything you need for that meeting is in this envelope. And, remember, she hasn't paid you anything yet. Then you have an appointment with a Mr. Jenkins at 10:30. He wants you to do some sleuthing concerning his business partner. Lunch is at the Gateway at 1 o'clock for the Citizens for Homeless Children group. Here are some notes for you concerning that. I've sorted through the mail. There were several bills and a check from the Glossar family for the work you did for them. I've already marked that paid in the ledger. Oh, and this looks like something personal."

She placed a regular-sized hand addressed envelope in front of Nash.

"Thanks, Anne. You know, you've been invaluable to me since you started here."

"I know," she said and continued organizing.

Nash smiled. That was Anne. Her comment was not haughty or self-gratifying. She dealt in facts. And the fact was that she had become indispensable to Nash and his personal investigator business. It was something they both recognized.

"I saw you talking with Professor Scutter last night after the lecture. Did you find out anything significant during the conversation?" Nash asked, opening the envelope.

"I found the whole thing extremely interesting," Anne replied. "I'm glad you asked me to go. The man is a wealth of knowledge. However, I don't know that I have any new information pertaining to the case."

Nash's face greyed.

"What? What is it?" Anne asked immediately.

"A second warning."

"A second warning? What does that mean?"

"I haven't told you, but while I was at the hospital Friday night, someone slashed one of my tires and left me a note telling me to quit snooping."

Anne gasped.

"Louie and Tony were the only people I told out of necessity. Tony discovered the extent of the tire damage when I took it to him for repair. I took the note to Louie to check it for fingerprints."

"And?"

"I haven't heard anything, yet. I just don't want Ma to know. She doesn't need to worry."

Nash decided he had better call and report this note to Louie, as well. Anne stood quietly in the background while he explained the details.

"Yeah? Okay. There's probably none on this one either. I can bring it by if you like. Actually, the exact same words as the first. Okay. Thanks."

"I don't like this," Anne frowned as he hung up. "If this is the second note, then our person is getting bolder, right?"

"That's a good thing," Nash replied. "That's when people begin to make mistakes."

Another phone call interrupted their conversation.

"Really? You again?" Anne heard Nash say. Then there was an agonizing pause while Nash listened and while Anne waited.

"Results are in from the poison in Holiday's system." Nash relayed when he hung up the phone.

"That's good news."

"It seems to be toxin from a plant common to Africa."

Nash pushed back from his desk and appeared to be in deep thought. Anne waited a few minutes before she spoke.

"And we both know who has been to Africa recently," she said.

←——————————→

His meeting at the Gateway finished in time for Nash to make another trip to the Season household. He was not at all comfortable with the information he had received from Louie. The task before him would not be an easy one, though. Somewhere between his office and the Season estate, Nash needed a good reason to be in Winter's writing den. Something he had read that afternoon when he had interviewed Winter kept nagging at him and continued to haunt him. It was something he had seen on a writing pad on Winter's desk. He could not remember the exact words, but now, he felt they might be important to the case.

Giles met him at the front door. Nash's presence surprised him.

"Is someone expecting you today?" he asked.

"No," Nash replied. "I just thought of something else I needed to talk with Winter about. Is she around?"

"I believe she just came in and is talking with her mother. I'll tell her you wish to speak with her."

"Would it be all right if I headed on up to her writing den and waited there?" Nash asked nervously.

After a few seconds of silence during which Nash held his breath, Giles finally answered.

"I suppose that would be all right."

While Giles went to find Winter, Nash bounded up the stairs. Luckily, the pad of paper was still on the desk. He hurriedly scanned the pages: "rich family," "poisoned mother," "large inheritance." His stomach began to churn as he scanned further. Was it the outline for a story or the blueprints for murder? His thoughts were interrupted by the sound of footsteps coming up the stairs. He quickly placed the pad back on the desk, moved to the window, and searched his mind for a plausible reason for his visit. He whirled around at the sound of her voice.

"Well, this is a pleasant surprise!" Winter greeted him.

"Yeah," Nash searched for words. "Just a couple of things that I wanted to clear up."

Winter smiled her beguiling smile as Nash struggled to conceal his true feelings. Then he looked out the window of the room—the one that overlooked the massive flower gardens and the gazebo.

"It's that motion camera," he blurted out. "That's bothered me ever since I was here last week. Does anyone ever monitor it?"

"I really don't know," Winter said as she joined him in looking out the window. "I suppose Summer does. She's the one who installed it. I've never seen her do it. But then, it's not like I spend a great amount of time thinking about it." She paused and frowned. "Is that the reason for your visit? If it is, you could go to Summer—"

"Oh, no," Nash struggled to recover. "I wanted to hear more about your trip to Africa. I was intrigued by the presentation last night."

Nash was relieved when Winter accepted his reason for being there and immediately began what turned into an hour of discussion about the trip. Nash listened carefully to each detail, realizing what might appear unimportant could easily become pertinent to the case. After a time, he said he wanted to speak with Summer and found her busy uncrating a new bird bath.

"Here, can I help you with that?" he offered as he saw the petite blonde struggling with the weight of the crate.

"I've got it," Summer replied, and Nash saw the determination on her face.

He did, however, help her remove the piece of molded concrete.

"Where does it go?" he asked.

She directed his path and together they put it in place.

"Thanks," she offered as she reached up to wipe a smudge from his face. "Did you come by just to help me unload this monstrosity?"

"Actually, I'm more interested in the motion camera you have installed on the end of the greenhouse. Do you ever monitor it?"

"Sometimes. If there's any damage done in the gardens, I will look to see if I'm contending with a deer or a groundhog or a raccoon. But I really haven't looked at it for quite some time mainly because there hasn't been any destruction lately. Why the interest?"

"I was wondering if it might have recorded anything on the night of the 10th."

"We can look and see," Summer told him. "I can set it up for you in the potting shed."

Nash was relieved that Summer had put aside her flirtatious manner to be serious for a time. He followed her to the potting shed and waited for her to set up the equipment so he could observe.

"There it is," Summer said. "This is the 10th of July. See, the date and time are in the corner. This controls the fast forward function, and this button will take you back, or you can press pause to freeze a frame. Sorry. I suppose you already know how to run these things. I've got some things to do. When you're done, just press this button, and the whole thing will shut down."

Nash thanked her and was relieved that she left him alone to watch the tape. He watched several minutes before anything came on the screen. His senses heightened when he saw a blurred figure hurrying through the flower gardens. He could not be sure, but it appeared the figure was carrying a rather large box. The figure wore a man's hat so the face was indistinguishable. Nash watched until the figure disappeared from the camera's view. Nash rewound the tape and watched it again and again. It looked like a small man, but then again, it could have been a woman. He squinted as he tried to find any clue to the person's identity, but the tape quality was poor.

Nash pushed play again. Suddenly, what appeared to be the same figure became visible again. Nash checked the time on the tape to make sure he was not watching the same moment over again. This was clearly a second incident. The time interval between the first sighting and second sighting was thirty-five minutes. Nash entered some pertinent information into his cell phone and reviewed the entire tape again just to make sure he was correct.

When Nash left the potting shed, he walked back to the house and attempted to trace the steps the figure on the tape had taken. He stopped at the corner of the potting shed, where the camera could no longer follow the person, and looked around. There was no place for an intruder to park a vehicle. There were no tire tracks. The area appeared to be undisturbed. There was just Giles' little house and an old abandoned shack.

The door to the shack creaked as Nash opened it. A quick look around told him that no one had been in the building for some time.

On his way back toward the house, he realized the back door to the greenhouse had been left ajar. After looking around to see if anyone was watching, he opened the screen door and ducked inside.

Nash glanced around the room. The only light came from the sky lights overhead. Not many plants were growing at this particular time. Instead, there were tables filled with empty containers and debris. Obviously, Summer had not had time to clean up the mess.

He saw nothing unusual at first. However, when he began to look underneath the tables, the light from his cell phone revealed some plastic totes that looked out of place. He pulled one of the containers out from under the table to get a closer look. He pried open the lid. Gold and glass glimmered in the light from the cell phone.

A noise from outside the greenhouse alerted Nash that someone was coming. He quickly closed the box and shoved it back into its place. He looked around for some place to hide when he heard someone at the door. He laid flat on the floor behind the tables as far away from the door as possible and prayed the intruder would not walk that way.

"Hmm! I must have forgotten to close the door," he heard Summer murmur.

Then he listened as he heard her close the door behind her. He breathed a sigh. Once he was sure he was alone, he crept from the greenhouse through the potting shed. After peering out the door and seeing no one, he ambled toward his car. He was relieved when he slid into the driver's seat.

New possibilities raced through his mind as he headed for town. It seemed Summer had become the number one suspect in the case.

12

←——————————————————————→

"It just doesn't make any sense," Nash told Anne as they once again poured over the facts diagrammed on the wall while sitting in Nash's office. "Why would Summer do such a thing?"

"Are you sure you're not letting your personal feelings get in the way?" Anne was blunt.

"I've thought about it. But, if she knew the camera would reveal that she had taken the items, why would she have consented to let me watch the video? And hiding the stolen items in the greenhouse just seems too convenient—they are right there where anyone might stumble across them. Why would she do that? Maybe someone is trying to frame her."

"You say you couldn't identify the person on the tape?"

"Beyond that the person was small, I could make out no other personal features. But then both Summer and Autumn are rather small. Plus, another thing that bothers me is some sketches I saw in Autumn's art studio. There was one of her with a man's hat shielding her face. When I saw the figure in the video, that picture came to mind. It strikes me as significant."

"So, now, essentially, we have Summer *and* Autumn as the most likely suspects."

"In that first interview with Summer, she indicated that Autumn was the biggest disappointment to her mother. Now, I wonder if she was trying to cast suspicion on her sister to protect herself."

"So, what are you going to do next? Are you going to tell Holly you found the items?"

"Not just yet. You know, Holly never said anything about me finding the items. She just wanted to know which daughter would have taken them."

"You're still convinced it had to be one of the four girls?"

"I don't have any reason to suspect anyone else at this time."

Just then the telephone rang.

"Nash here."

Nash suddenly sat in an upright position as he listened intently.

"Really!…That changes everything. This is not the open and shut case I thought it would be…Well, thanks for the info."

Nash hung up the receiver and sat staring at the phone while Anne waited.

"What? What is it?"

"That was Louie. Results came back from the state lab. They found more specific information about the poison. It is something from—guess what—South Africa! The exact area Winter had visited. Louie's sending me the details. I can't pronounce the scientific name, but something about sore-eye flower. Causes colic, tremors, abdominal discomfort, and hallucinations."

Both Anne and Nash sat in silence. Finally, Anne spoke.

"Guess that puts Winter at the top of the list again," she said.

⟵——————————⟶

Not many students were on the college campus during the summer session. It was not difficult for Nash to locate Professor Scutter's laboratory in the Science Department. The professor was bent over a microscope on a lab table, jotting notes on a clip board. He was so intent on his work that he did not notice Nash's presence.

"Professor Scutter?" Nash said softly so as not to startle the scientist.

When he got no response, he repeated the greeting a little louder each time. It took three times of Nash raising his voice for the professor to acknowledge Nash's presence.

"Oh," the professor turned, "I thought I was alone. How can I help you?"

Nash stifled a grin. Indeed, he was alone in his thoughts.

"My name is Nash Adams. I was at your lecture the other evening and found it quite stimulating, especially the part about the uses of herbs and berries and things like that. I've recently heard about something called a sore-eye flower. I was wondering if perhaps you had come across it in your travels and if you could tell me anything about it."

"Ah, yes," Professor Scutter said as he removed his glasses. "*Boophone disticha* or its common names include sore-eye flower and Cape poison bulb. Very dangerous when ingested or when it gets into the blood stream. However, the natives in certain parts of South Africa use it for various things. It is used by many Bushmen as an ingredient in poison arrows for hunting, but it is also used as a poultice that is accredited with having pain relieving attributes when applied to wounds. Some even use it to drive out evil spirits from a person, but that remedy is frequently fatal. Symptoms of ingesting it include gastrointestinal distress, intoxication, disorientation, hallucinations, and these are present in those who receive it as part of some native treatment. Other symptoms can be tremors and death."

"So, it's lethal?"

"It can be. When dealing with any organic medicine, environmental conditions under which it is grown can make a difference in its toxicity. If enough of it is ingested, death is always a possibility, and for this particular plant, it does not take much to have that effect. Although some natives think it cures stomach problems, I believe it actually can increase them."

"What if it was administered in very small doses? Could the side effects be minimal? And wouldn't that make it more difficult to detect?"

The professor was quiet while he thought. "It would require a very minute dose, but I suppose that is possible."

"One other thing—is it difficult to obtain? I mean, can just anyone purchase it? And how would one go about getting it?"

"My boy, we live in an age when anything can be purchased for the right price."

"Thank you, Professor," Nash nodded as he stood and shook the professor's hand. "You've been very helpful."

Nash began to put some things together in his mind as he headed once more toward the Season estate to search for the plant that he had found a picture of on the Internet in the gardens. He was so lost in his thoughts as he approached it that he almost missed the significance of the vehicle coming toward him. Suddenly, his mind jolted to what Winter had told him. Giles' means of transportation was taxi cab. Niles had just passed a taxi cab coming from the direction of the Season property and could think of no other reason for one to be this far out of town. He made a U-turn and followed it at a safe distance. When he came to a passing zone, he sped up and passed the cab so he could read the writing on its side. Sure enough, it was Harold's Taxi Service—the same company Winter had said Giles used.

Nash was not sure, but he thought he had seen Giles in the back seat, too. Nash turned onto a side road and waited for the cab to pass before he pulled out and continued to follow it. It was a weak lead, but it could be a lead in the case.

Although some might find the life of a private investigator exciting, there were times when it was quite boring. It was always a challenge, however, to follow someone without being detected. Nash lagged behind the taxi cab to keep from arousing suspicions.

Its first stop was a grocery store. Seeing the old man exit the cab and walk into the store confirmed Nash's suspicions that it was indeed Giles. Nash wondered if Mrs. Snook had asked for an ingredient for her cooking. After the grocery store, the cab entered city traffic, it drove straight to the library. Nash waited half a block down the street for what seemed like an hour while Giles was inside. So did the taxi cab driver. Finally, Giles emerged through the library doors with a stack of books under his arm.

The cab's next stop was a local diner. Again, the driver of the taxi waited. Nash wondered if Giles were meeting someone. Nash needed to know that information. He got out of the car and entered the restaurant with his head down. He quickly scanned the area and noticed Giles sitting at a table all alone with his back toward the door. Nash slipped unnoticed onto one of the stools at the counter. From that vantage point, he could see Giles' image reflected in the mirror on the wall behind the counter.

"What'll you have?" the waitress asked as she swiped a wet cloth over the counter in front of him.

"Pepsi, please. Easy on the ice."

"That it?"

"Yeah, that will be all."

Seconds later, the drink was in front of him.

"Thanks, Susie," Nash noticed her name on her uniform. Susie smiled in return.

Nash continued watching as Giles finished his food and lingered over a cup of coffee. When he saw the old gentleman push the coffee cup aside and wipe his mouth, Nash covered the side of his own face with his hand just in case Giles might recognize him. He heard Giles exchange pleasantries with Susie at the cash register and then the tingling of the bell on the door as he left the diner. Putting some cash on the counter and nodding at Susie, Nash hurried to his car in time to see the taxi pulling out of the parking lot.

It was not difficult to keep track of the taxi even with city traffic. The driver proved to be conservative—or else he was getting paid by the minute. Giles' final stop was the post office. Nash parked down the street and waited. Finally, Giles emerged with a small package under his arm. Nash followed the cab a little longer. When he realized it was moving north out of town, he concluded it was probably going back to the Season estate. He knew he had business there, but he wanted to finish this lead before checking out that one. He turned his Chevy around and headed back into town to talk with Susie at the restaurant.

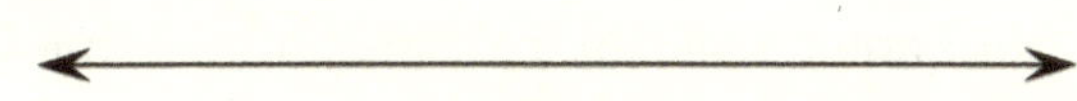

Business at the restaurant had slowed to a crawl by the time Nash got back to the city and the parking lot was almost empty. Susie looked up from filling paper napkin dispensers when she saw him enter. She smiled.

"Back so soon?" she grinned. "That must have been a really good Pepsi."

Nash blushed to think she had remembered. But he saw it as a good sign. Susie had a mind for detail. That was probably why she was a good waitress—and why she might possibly be of help to Nash.

"Yeah, I'd like another Pepsi, but do you have a minute?" Nash asked.

"Sure. Have a seat."

Nash sat down across the table from her as Susie went to grab the drink and continued her work.

"I have a couple of questions," he began. "If you can remember that I ordered a Pepsi, I'm sure you know all your customers pretty well. There was a gentleman who was here earlier—part of the lunch crowd. He sat at that booth over there by the window."

"Oh, sure," she said, glancing at the booth. "You know, most people are creatures of habit. If they're regulars, they tend to sit in the same places."

"Is he a regular?"

"He has been recently, say for the last several months or so. Before that, it was only once in a while, but now it's been every week."

"Can you tell me anything else about him? Does he engage you in conversation?"

Susie frowned. "You a cop or something? Is he in trouble?"

"No, but I am a personal investigator," Nash told her as he produced one of his cards. "And no, I don't believe he's in trouble. I just need to follow up on every possible lead."

"I knew it. I told Cindy after you left that I thought you'd come in for more than just a Pepsi, easy on the ice."

"Maybe you should go into the investigating business." Nash laughed.

Susie smiled in return.

"Well, all I know is that his name is Giles, and he must work for some rich people. I don't know if they don't pay him much or it's just his way, but he seems to be very frugal with his money. Actually, he has talked a lot about money lately. I just thought he was trying to get out of leaving a tip. Anyway, he seems to be concerned about having enough money. And, one other thing—he's been very nervous the last couple of weeks. If I had to guess, I'd say he's keeping a secret or hiding something. Just a feeling I got."

"Is he always alone? Does he ever meet anyone else here?"

"Umm, not that I remember."

"Susie, you have been most helpful. I'd appreciate it if you didn't mention this to anyone."

"Gee, I hope the little man didn't do anything wrong. He seems like an okay guy."

"Well, let's hope that is the case. Thanks for your time."

Nash slid some money across the table to her.

"Oh, that's not necessary," she said with a glint in her eye. "I'm glad to help out a handsome guy trying to right the wrongs of society."

Nash smiled and left the diner. Next step—Harold's Taxi Service.

Nash was pretty sure Harold had enough time to deliver Giles back to the Season estate and return to the city, so he headed over to the taxi cab company. He was right. He found Harold's cab parked in front of a small store front. Apparently, Harold did not get much business. Lettering on a window, filmy with dirt, announced that this was indeed the taxi service. Nash had to push hard on the door to open it and then slam it shut behind him. The space was no bigger than 12' x 12'. There was just enough room for Nash to stand between the door and the wooden counter. Gouges in the well-worn counter top peeked out from underneath stacks of papers. Harold sat to one side in a broken-down, over-stuffed chair. He struggled to get out of it as Nash entered.

"How can I help you?" Harold asked as he moved to present a more professional appearance from behind the counter.

"Just looking for some information."

Harold appeared to be uneasy at Nash's remark.

"My license is all up to date," Harold said nervously swallowing.

"Oh, I'm not here about that," Nash reassured him. "I believe you have what you might refer to as a standing customer, and I have some questions concerning him."

"Well, I can't give out information about my people. That's private information." Harold seemed offended that Nash would ask him to do such a thing.

"I understand. I'm a friend of Mrs. Season, and she is concerned about her employee, Giles. I was just wondering if you've noticed anything different about Giles, lately. He's getting along in age, you know. If something's going on with him, she would like to know."

Harold squinted at Nash for a brief time before he answered.

"Nah, I ain't noticed anything. I pick him up every Wednesday, and he pretty much has the same routine. Been doin' it for years."

"Nothing has changed recently?"

"No," Harold hesitated. "Well, a few months ago he added a regular stop at the post office, and once I took him to the community college."

"Do you know what that's about? Was he interested in taking a class there? I mean, does he ever talk about it?"

"No, can't say as he has. He sometimes talks about having enough money to retire on. Other than that, he don't talk much."

"Thank you. I appreciate your time."

Nash turned to leave, but then stopped.

"One more question—have you ever noticed anything about the package he gets at the post office?"

"Nope. It's always just a small package."

"Thanks again. And Mrs. Season would appreciate it if you didn't discuss our conversation with Giles. She doesn't want him to feel uncomfortable that she was checking up on him."

Harold nodded, and Nash headed back to his office.

"Hey, boss, I didn't expect you back in the office today," Anne greeted Nash teasingly as he came through the door.

"Just adding some information to the wall," he commented.

"You look like you had a good day."

"I spent part of the day with Professor Scutter and part of it tailing Giles."

"And?"

"I found out a lot from the professor. Nothing significant about Giles, though. Mostly routine stuff."

"You found out anything useful?"

"Maybe. I think I know more about the poison that is making Holly sick. Plus," he added as he stared at the wall, "I'm pretty sure we can eliminate Autumn from the list of suspects—she would not have access to or knowledge about plants. Plus, she was inside the hospital when my tires were slashed. We could probably eliminate Spring, too. She would have access to poisons, but not plants. Plus, her entire career would be in jeopardy. I'm pretty sure she wouldn't risk that."

"So, we're back to Winter and Summer," Anne stated.

"Okay, let's talk about Winter. What do we know?"

"We know she has recently made a trip to Africa and the poisonous material Holly had in her body is found in Africa."

"Yes, but the professor told me in this day and age it would be easy to buy it."

Anne frowned.

"So, are you saying that anyone could have access to it?"

"Pretty much. But the lab said specifically southern Africa so that must mean they can tell the difference as to where it was grown."

"That puts Winter up there as number one suspect again."

"Not necessarily. While we know Winter was in Africa, we also know someone who is familiar with growing plants and who could have had one shipped in from there."

"Summer," Anne sighed.

"I need to search the property to see if Summer might be harvesting the stuff," Nash concluded.

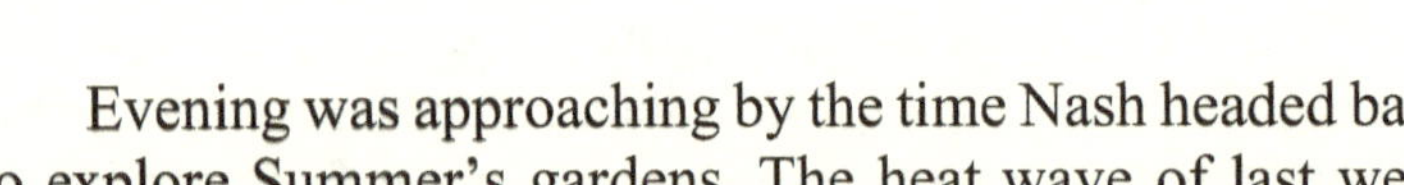

Evening was approaching by the time Nash headed back to explore Summer's gardens. The heat wave of last week seemed to have worn itself out, and a light breeze rippled through the tops of the trees. It had been a full day with still no definitive answers to a lot of questions. Sounds coming from the pool indicated Winter was taking an evening swim. He found Summer near the potting shed. She was struggling with a wheel barrow full of soil.

"Can I help you with that?" he asked.

"Oh, you startled me," she answered, wiping the perspiration from her face. "What are you? Superman? Arriving at just the right time to save the damsel in distress?"

"I don't claim to be Superman. Are you in distress?'

"Seems like I'm always struggling with something when you drop by. I'm a little surprised you're here. Or did you just find another excuse to see me?"

She smiled coyly as she noticed the red color creep across his face.

"I thought I'd like to ask you some questions," he said, trying to ignore her comment. "Some questions about plants."

"What? You're suddenly interested in horticulture?"

"You might say that."

"Okay, shoot. I'll tell you what I know," she agreed. "And what I don't know, I'll make up."

Seeing the perplexed look on his face, she continued, "Oh, don't do that. I can't stand sad faces. I was only joking. What is it you want to know?"

"I'd like for you to take me through your gardens and tell me about the plants there. I'm specifically interested in any plant that might have medicinal value."

Summer frowned as a puzzled look spread across her face. But she walked him through the gardens, explaining each plant as they went.

"A lot of plants were common medicines for our ancestors," she told him. "I really don't know a lot about it. But here is chamomile. You probably recognize that it is used in teas for relaxation. I have feverfew and rosemary. I think both of those have medicinal value. And I grow garlic and have aloe. Both of those have multiple uses. As I said before, I'm not an expert on their uses."

As they walked around, Nash kept his eye open for the flowering plant he had researched.

"You seem preoccupied," Summer noted. "In fact, you don't even seem interested in these plants you wanted to see."

"Sorry. I guess I am a bit distracted."

"Does this have something to do with Holly's incident? Are you getting close to solving this case?"

Nash turned to look into her tanned face. The bright sun glistened in her eyes.

"Yes, I think I'm getting close."

"Good," she said. "Now, if you don't mind, I have a delivery truck to meet."

Nash stood there for a while after she left once again scanning the gardens for anything remarkable. Once he was certain the plant he was looking for was not there, he decided the only remarkable things at the Season house were the four young women who lived there.

# 13

← ──────────────── →

"I think I have it figured out," Nash told Louie as they sat across from each other in the police office break room.

Nash shared his suspicions with Louie as he frequently did when working on a case.

"That certainly sounds reasonable as far as suspicions go," Louie agreed, "but I don't think there's enough there to obtain a search warrant."

Nash nodded in agreement. Of course, he was disappointed. There was a short period of silence while each young man searched for a solution to the problem. Then Nash sat up in his chair with yet another idea.

"What if," he began, "we see if we can flush out the person responsible? Pretend we know a little bit more than we actually know. Maybe he or she will fold under the pressure."

"Now you're on to something," Louie agreed. "That just might work. It's not like we're dealing with professional criminals. Why don't you set up a meeting with everyone? I'll be there, too, and that will add some authority to the situation. What do you think?"

"I think that's a great idea. I'll get in touch with Holly right away and see how quickly we can do it."

"The sooner the better. I don't want to give the culprit time to think and make a plan. Get back to me when you know something."

"Will do."

As Nash was leaving, Louie called out from his desk, "Decline the whole thing if she invites us to dinner."

Nash still had a smile on his face as he bolted down the stairs and dialed Holly's number.

Nash could tell by the tone of her voice that Holly was pleased that he called.

"How are you feeling?" he asked.

"Actually, much better," she confirmed. "Perhaps is was some tainted food after all."

"Actually, that's why I'm calling. I think I have some information for you. I believe we can wrap up this mystery. But I'd like to meet with all of you as soon as possible."

"All of us?"

"Yes. You, the girls, Mrs. Snook, Giles, and Mr. Wainwright. It would be helpful if all are present."

"That does leave me a bit curious," Holly was hesitant. "But I will see what I can arrange and get back to you."

"Remember—the sooner, the better. We don't want the person involved to cover any tracks," Nash emphasized.

"I'll be in touch."

Nash sat in his Chevy with his cell phone in his hand, pleased at his progress.

Holly was prompt in responding to Nash's request. A meeting was in place for the following evening—Thursday. Nash was confident in the plan as he edged through town traffic toward the Season estate. Louie would arrive just a few minutes behind him. As he drove, Nash thought about each of the girls and what their reaction to the evening might be.

It had been almost two weeks since Nash made his first visit to the mansion, that fateful evening when Holly had her initial poisoning episode at the dinner table. And now Nash thought he had the answer to her problems—or perhaps his discoveries would only add to her problems. Whatever happened, the plan was in place, and if it worked, the mystery of the missing antiques and Holly's medical issues would both be resolved.

Just then, his cell phone rang and interrupted his thoughts.

"Hey," he said as Katie's face appeared on the screen. "What's up?"

"This call may be monitored for training purposes," the voice said. "You have won first place in our latest contest."

"But I haven't entered any contests," Nash played along with the game.

"Your name has been selected from a list of names of prominent young men of Mason County."

"Oh, really? Just what prize have I won?"

"Dinner for two at the Gateway Restaurant."

"I see," Nash was beginning to understand. "And how do I claim this prize?"

"Well, first of all, you have to find just the right young lady with whom to share the dinner."

"Hmm, it has to be female?"

"Well, it doesn't have to be, but that would be the preferred companion."

"I'll think on it. But right now, I'm on my way to solve a very important case."

"Actually, that's why I called," Katie was serious now. "I didn't know if you had heard the latest weather bulletin, but the weather is going to turn really bad. They are predicting storms with rain and high winds. I just thought I should warn you. They say Mason County is going to be the hardest hit."

Nash leaned forward to check the sky through his windshield.

"Looks like the clouds are starting to gather," he told Katie. "Don't worry. I won't take any unnecessary chances."

"Okay, take care."

He heard the concern in her voice.

"Oh, hey, about that dinner—I think I just figured out who I might invite."

"Yeah?"

"Yeah. My mom could sure use a night out," he laughed.

"You're impossible!" Katie replied, joining him in his laughter.

"I love you, Katie," Nash whispered.

"I love you, too. Be safe," she responded.

After hanging up, Nash tried to get some weather information on the radio as he drove. A major storm was indeed approaching Mason County and would probably hit between the hours of 10:00 and midnight.

The sky had turned dark by the time he arrived at the Season estate. He entered the mansion to find everyone already assembled just as he had requested. Holly was seated at the head of the dining room table just as she had been almost two weeks ago. Although a bit pale, she still reflected her image of control. Attorney Wainwright was seated at her right, looking a bit uncomfortable at having been asked to attend such a meeting. Seated immediately left of Holiday was the shy, beautiful, and somewhat mysterious Autumn. She seemed so vulnerable to Nash. Her face reflected her artistic side as the subtlety of her makeup blended with the peach print blouse she wore. She nervously played with her auburn hair.

Giles and Mrs. Snook were seated between Autumn and Winter. As usual, Giles wore little expression on his face, and Mrs. Snook nervously rubbed her hands together. Nash expected her to break out in tears at any minute.

Winter seemed agitated, something Nash found to be a bit unusual for her. In his past interactions with her, she was always in control of herself and her surroundings. The tips of her dark hair were damp, so he suspected that she had recently come from the swimming pool. She looked intently into his face and then looked away as if she were embarrassed by what she might be feeling. She absently played with the silver heart she wore on a chain around her neck.

As Nash took the empty seat at the end of the table, he looked at Spring who frowned a bit from her seat across the table from Winter. He briefly pondered the reason for that. He wondered if she were afraid he would reveal something she had told him during their private conversations. Spring tapped her foot impatiently.

Summer was the last figure at the table, sitting next to Mr. Wainwright. She looked up at him with her brown eyes that seemed to plead with him. Her tan face was framed with her short blonde hair. He looked into her adorable face and realized how attached he had become to her these last two weeks. However bold she had been at times, she still had that little girl innocence about her that made him want to protect her. Still, the time had come when he could not protect any of them. This night would change someone's life forever.

"Thank you all for coming," he began. "Hopefully, by the end of tonight some questions will be answered." Nash was aware that all eyes were on him except for one person. "Detective Louie, who was here the night Holly had the medical incident, will be here shortly to help explain things."

A murmur spread around the table. Nash ignored it and continued.

"I hear there's a storm coming through our area tonight, so I would like to keep this as brief as possible."

Just then the doorbell rang, and Giles excused himself to answer it. In a few seconds, Louie followed the servant into the dining room. Louie nodded to the group in greeting.

"The wind has picked up, and the rain has started," he said, shaking some water from his jacket. Giles quickly took it from him so he did not create a mess. "It's gonna be a bad one, they say."

Nash motioned for Louie to take a seat between Summer and Spring after thanking him for coming.

"Let me start by saying that the antiques that were taken from the house never left the property."

Expressions of surprise crept across everyone's faces as the group exchanged glances and murmurs.

"As you know, I was hired to try to find out which one of you stole the articles in question. I was surprised to find that each one of the girls had both the motive and the opportunity to commit the crime," Nash began. "As we know, two crimes have now been committed here. When Holly hired me, my job was to find out who had stolen the antiques from the house. When Holly was poisoned, I was planted in the center of a second crime to investigate. I believe I have found enough information to connect the two together.

"As each of the girls pointed out, it wouldn't make sense for them to take the antiques. After all, everything in the house will eventually be theirs. Is that not true, Mr. Wainwright?"

"Yes," Mr. Wainwright agreed uncomfortably. "According to the terms of the will, they all will inherit equally."

"It is not my job to protect any one of you. My job is to find out the truth. At one time or another during my investigation, I believed any one of you could have been guilty. Each one of you has suffered because of the conditions governing this household. Being set free from the bonds that have constrained you is reason enough for motive.

Yet, each one of you girls expressed a fondness for your mother and for each other. Although you all hide your feelings, it was apparent when I talked with you. I can say the same thing about your feelings for your father even though it is the very terms of his will that keep you confined here. I'm not sure that I understand the significance behind those terms. Could you enlighten us further on that, Mr. Wainwright?"

Mr. Wainwright cleared his throat after sending a furtive glance toward Holly. "The terms of the will are clear and concise. Stormy established them when he was alive, and his dear wife has continued his wishes. Believe me when I say that they are in the girls' best interest."

Both Louie and Nash noted that Mr. Wainwright's response was evasive concerning the question. Nash chose to ignore that and proceed.

"Spring, at one time, you were my prime suspect. Not for taking the antiques but for the poisoning. After all, you have access to many drugs. But I also know, after talking with Mrs. Snook, that you are seldom in the kitchen and therefore it would be unlikely for you to have an opportunity to add poison to food unnoticed. Although you feel as if your mother looks down on you because of your profession, I sense that you are fulfilled through your work. Plus, you continue to live here even though you alone could support yourself. I believe living here would be your choice even if the clause was not in the will. You have a sense of family.

"Autumn, you were next on my list, mostly because of your artistic nature. You feel things more deeply than some. At the same time, you seldom leave the house. I was confused by the similarity between a self-portrait in your room that seemed to match the figure that the garden's camera caught stealing the items, but that proved to be only coincidence. I have now concluded that you are content being an artist. I do want you to know there is good reason for your mother to have special feelings toward you and toward your chosen field of art despite her vocal disdain about it. Ask her sometime about her own pursuits as a college student. I think the two of you have more in common than you thought. And as far as the poisoning goes, I have concluded that the thought would never occur to you nor would you have access to the poison."

Nash felt a rush of uncomfortableness as he launched into his thoughts about Summer. He cleared his throat as he regarded the helpless-looking young woman.

"Summer, you were the prime suspect from the beginning. You are the rebel of the family. You represent the farthest thing from what your family stands for. You also keep your feelings locked inside a flirtatious shell. It took me a long time to realize how deeply you feel about things and that was one reason for me to suspect you. Despite your outward appearance, you really do care. I apologize for exposing that. You've done a really good job of concealing it over the years. However, I had good reason to suspect you. Mrs. Snook told me you liked baking for the holidays, which moved you up on the scale of suspicion because it gave you access to food. The potting shed contains all kinds of chemicals that could easily have been used for poisoning, and your garden contains plants that might have poison inside them. Finally, when my tire was slashed, you were the first person I thought of."

"What?" Holly interrupted. "What tire? This is the first I've heard of that."

"It happened during your second trip to the hospital," Nash explained. "When I left you, I found one of my tires damaged. When I thought about it afterward, I recalled seeing Summer's truck parked nearby. To make it even more suspicious, Summer was the only one who wasn't already at the hospital when I arrived, so she would have had the perfect opportunity, the tools, and the know-how to accomplish it."

Summer looked at Nash with fear in her eyes.

"But you didn't commit any of the crimes," Nash concluded.

Summer's brown eyes filled with tears as she looked at him. Instead of seeing the incredible flirt she had been, Nash saw a loving, caring person.

"The state lab has now identified the source of the substance used to poison the food. We know it is indeed deliberate poisoning."

Again, there was a murmur in response to that information.

"That brings us to Winter," Nash continued as he turned toward the oldest Season daughter. Disbelief appeared on the faces around the table. All eyes were on Winter as Nash continued. "Winter, you also have risen to the top of the list so many times! From the first time I met you, I knew you were not the least bit intimidated by your mother. In many ways, you have been the perfect choice as a suspect. You had opportunity because you were here during the times when the antiques were taken and your mother was poisoned. You love to cook, so you had access to the kitchen, and it would not be unusual for you to be doing something in there. I saw the notes on your desk that described either a plot for a story or a plot for murder. When the results came back from the lab showing the poison in your mother's body had come from Africa, I was sure it was you. You learned a lot about native African customs and herbology when you were there. I heard you talk about ways the natives used different plants and leaves for medicinal purposes. I knew that anything you might not know your colleague, Professor Scutter, would know."

All the time Nash was talking, Louie was carefully watching the expressions on each face around the table.

"No! That's not possible!" Summer broke out as she stood in protest. "My sister is not capable of doing such a thing!"

"Perhaps we could take a break and have some refreshment, Nash," Holly suggested. "This has been so intense."

Mrs. Snook immediately excused herself to go to the kitchen. Giles followed her while the girls consoled each other in quiet whispers. Nash felt entirely isolated from them. Soon Giles and Mrs. Snook returned with a tray of glasses, a pitcher of iced lemonade and a smaller teapot with hot tea for Holly. There was a platter of shortbread cookies as well. Mrs. Snook went out of her way to assure everyone that they were okay to eat.

"I've hid them in a special place since I baked them," she stated.

Once drinks were served, Nash continued.

"No, Winter, it is not you. You did not take the antiques or try to poison your mother."

A sigh of relief was heard around the table. Holly seemed relived but equally perplexed. She had been certain that one of her daughters had taken the antiques. However, Nash had cleared each one.

"Nash, can I pour you some lemonade to drink?" Holly asked.

Nash moved quickly to the other end of the table where Holly sat poised with the pitcher of lemonade.

"Actually, I think I'd like to try some of your tea," he said calmly.

"Of course," Holly agreed. "Giles, would you pour Mr. Adams a cup of tea?"

The cup and saucer shook in Giles' hand as he lifted the teapot.

"Have you had the tremors long?" Nash said openly.

Giles glared at Nash.

"Or are you just nervous?" Nash prodded.

"This entire thing has made me extremely nervous," Giles answered.

"Why is that?" Nash continued.

"I have been in this family for years. I've watched these girls grow up. They are special to me. To think that one of them…well, it just seems an impossibility."

Giles passed the cup of hot tea to Nash. Nash studied Giles' face before he raised the cup to his lips. Giles' body tensed. Instead of taking a sip, Nash continued.

"Well, Giles, it turns out that it was an impossibility. None of the girls took the antiques, and none of them tried to poison their mother. Let me tell you a little bit more about the poison. Although it comes from Africa, we have access to similar products here in the States because of the Internet. It was a puzzle to me for a long time as to why someone would go to the trouble to purchase a product from Africa when there were so many other poisons available that would be easier to access. Of course, the obvious answer was to cast suspicion on someone else. That someone just happened to be the person who had recently come back from Africa. Actually, I think that was what prompted the whole idea."

Nash raised the cup of tea to his lips and blew a bit on the surface, ready to sip the tea. Just then, a huge clap of thunder shook the room, and the lights blinked for a second.

"No!" Giles shouted in agony. "Don't drink it."

Gasps of surprise echoed around the table.

"Why shouldn't I drink it?" Nash asked. "Will I exhibit some of the same signs as Holly had?"

"I confess," Giles began to cry. "I did it."

Everyone sat in a stupor of disbelief. Finally, Holly rose to her feet and came to him.

"Why, Giles?" she said quietly. "Why did you feel the need? Weren't you happy here?"

"That was just it. This was my home. I have been here all my life."

"Yes, of course, and it would continue to be your home. We would be your family forever."

"You don't understand," Giles said through his tears. "I knew what was about to happen. I knew you were going to put me out with no place to go and nothing to sustain me in my remaining years."

"Whatever are you talking about?" Holly was puzzled.

"I think you and Mr. Wainwright have some things to discuss with the girls," Nash interrupted. "It's time they were made aware of the circumstances. Giles, you will have to go with Detective Louie here."

Louie stepped forward, and Giles did not resist. His head was bowed in shame and remorse.

"I'm so sorry. I'm so sorry," Giles kept repeating as Louie led him out into the stormy night and into the police car for the trip to the police station.

Nash looked around at those remaining at the table. Clearly, all were disturbed by the revelation that their beloved butler was the culprit.

"I'm going to be leaving, now," Nash said. "I believe you all have a lot to talk about."

As Nash reached the foyer, he turned to take one last look at the Season family. He saw an exchange of hugs. He saw a compassionate mother with her beautiful daughters. Just as Nash reached for the door handle, he heard Mr. Wainwright begin his explanation about their real circumstances.

Nash was immediately met with a blast of wind and rain when he opened the door. It stung his face as he ran for the Chevy. Once in the safety of the car, he found a towel to wipe his head and face. The storm had indeed made its way into Mason County.

He started the car and turned on the windshield wipers full force as he crept slowly down the driveway. He strained to see the iron gate and gingerly pulled out onto the highway. Rain gushed in torrents across the road before him. Light from his headlights glared on the wet pavement. While the downpour blurred his vision, the winds played havoc with the Chevy. Nash fought to keep the car moving down the highway, moving toward the safety of home, but inside he was calm—satisfied at being able to bring the Seasons together again.

# 14

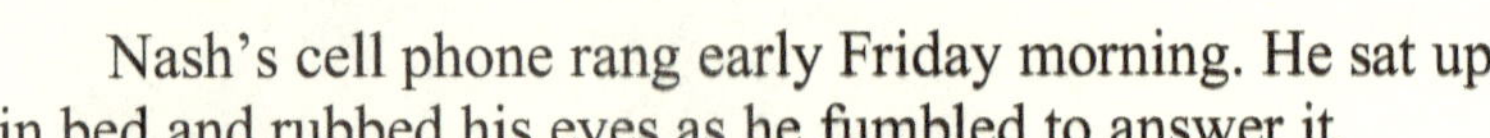

Nash's cell phone rang early Friday morning. He sat up in bed and rubbed his eyes as he fumbled to answer it.

"Hello."

"Buddy, I hate to tell you this—after all our hard work—we got major damage."

"What?" Nash was still trying to wake up.

"Damage from the storm last night. It's not good. We were taking calls all night with storm related problems. I tried to wait 'til you were awake."

"I'm awake now. Really bad, huh?"

Now, Nash was on his feet, rubbing his hand through his unruly hair as he paced his bedroom floor.

"Bad. I'll meet you down at the property before I go downtown to work. You need to see this for yourself."

"I'm on my way."

Nash struggled into his clothes. He drove in the early morning first rays of light. Damage from the storm was evident everywhere. He drove around tree trunks and debris that blocked streets. There were downed power lines to avoid. Luckily the neighborhood was not awake yet. He saw houses with missing parts and branches that looked as if they were growing through windows. Nash swallowed hard as he thought about possible loss of life.

When he reached Ella's Place, Louie was already there. Nash got slowly out of his car and stood beside his old friend as his mind tried to comprehend the magnitude of the disaster. Everywhere he looked, he saw more damage. A huge tree had fallen right on top of the unfinished building.

Other trees were either completely down or damaged. Only one sturdy oak and a few maples were left standing. The playground swings were twisted and mangled. The basketball backstop had been distorted beyond belief. The foul-ball net for the softball diamond had been blown to the far end of the property and looked like an oversized spider web covering some bushes. A mangled maze of leaves, twigs, and branches obscured the property.

"It makes me sick," Nash muttered softly.

"Sometimes I question why things happen the way they do," Louie mused.

"All the hard work we put in."

"And the work of others."

"And others," Nash agreed.

The two stood quietly for some time.

"I got to get to work," Louie finally said. "Meet you here early tomorrow?"

"Yeah. Tomorrow we'll start the cleanup here."

The two friends walked back to their vehicles with the weight of the disaster full on their shoulders.

"Everything go okay at the Season house after I left last night?" Louie asked.

"Yeah. When I left, they were kind of reuniting as a family, I think. How did it go with Giles?"

"Full confession. I'll send you a copy once it's printable."

"Good. I'll be at the office most of the day. See you in the morning."

$\longleftrightarrow$

Nash had little enthusiasm to finish the paperwork for the case. Instead, he spent some time talking with Mr. Meijer after he arrived at the deli. Mr. Meijer, in his own old-world way, had a calming effect on Nash. Perhaps it was the absence of his own father that caused Nash to find comfort in Mr. Meijer's words.

"Come sit down," Mr. Meijer said as he saw Nash enter. "I've just made a new pot of coffee."

Mr. Meijer saw the stress written across his tenant's face as he seated himself across a small table from Nash and pushed a cup of steaming coffee and a napkin-wrapped fresh pastry in front of him.

"How are things?" Mr. Meijer asked.

"You heard about the storm?"

"I heard it on the radio."

"It came straight through Ella's Place. Pretty much everything is ruined."

"I'm so sorry," Mr. Meijer said in genuine concern. "I know how much hard work you've put into it."

Nash nodded in agreement. "Not just me," he said. "A lot of people helped. I was so excited to think that we were making a difference."

"I understand. And I think you've already made a difference. It was your idea—your dream. Yours and policeman Louie. That makes it special."

Nash nodded again and played with the spoon in his cup of coffee.

"It's a hard thing," Mr. Meijer said with a great deal of sympathy. "It was always hard for my family. My father and mother experienced so much persecution in the old country and prejudice when they came to this country. I was only a lad, but I felt their pain just as I also felt their excitement when they were able to start a new life here in America. No matter how great the persecution was, father could always find something positive. I can remember him telling me that material things were good because they were a part of our dreams, but things could be taken from us. No one could take away our spirit. That was something we either kept or gave up on our own."

Tears formed in Mr. Meijer's eyes as he thought about everything his family had suffered.

"And now, look. I am the proud owner of my own delicatessen," he said with renewed spirit. "My father would be so proud of me—and so proud of his granddaughter, Anne. My regret is that he is no longer around to witness our accomplishments. Yet, his words remain in my heart."

Nash nodded, choking back some tears of his own.

"Do not worry, Mr. Nash. You will rebuild. Who knows? Perhaps the Name above us has a greater plan."

"Thank you, Mr. Meijer," Nash said gratefully. "You are always an inspiration to me."

"So, what are your plans for the park?"

Nash loved to hear the sounds of Mr. Meijer's broken English. It had a delightful and soothing ring to it.

"Tomorrow we will rebuild," Nash said with renewed confidence of his own. "Tomorrow, we start over again."

"Good boy," Mr. Meijer concluded.

He rose from his chair with a spring in his step, this interesting little man. He would go back to preparing food for his customers. He would listen to their stories with his usual interest. Later, he would share the day's events with his wife. He would sleep next to her at night. They would talk about all their blessings—the business, their wonderful Anne—and they would be grateful for it all.

"Take your time with the coffee," Mr. Meijer said as he shuffled off to meet his day. Then, turning, he added with pride, "I will make sandwiches today for you to take with you tomorrow. The Meijer Delicatessen will provide food at noon tomorrow for the workers."

Once again, Nash's eyes filled with tears as he mounted the steps that led to his office above the deli. His heart was filled with love and hope.

Once in his office, Nash spent some time studying the wall of information. The Season case had been an interesting one. He was glad he had made the acquaintance of the Season family. He smiled as he thought about each one of the people when he looked at the photos on the wall. That was how Anne found him when she came into work.

"Morning, boss," she said quietly.

Nash nodded. Then, putting his thoughts aside, he sat upright in his chair and began to scribble on a pad of paper. The Season case may have been closed, but he had things to do. He had ideas now, and he had phone calls to make.

"I didn't expect to see you so happy," Anne observed. "I heard about what happened with the storm. I'm sorry."

"Me, too. It's going to take a lot of work to get it all cleaned up, but we can do it."

"You sound determined."

"I have a lot of special people who give me inspiration."

Anne thought it best not to proceed with that line of thinking.

"How did it go last night?"

"It went fine. Giles confessed when he thought I was going to drink some of the tea."

"So, your little scheme worked, then."

"Yep. Sure did."

"And what if it hadn't? Did you have a backup plan?"

"Truthfully, no. I just knew it was him, and he would break sooner or later. Of course, if he hadn't, I would have had to confront him openly. I think he's truly sorry he did it."

"I guess that means I can start taking down the information wall?"

"Sure," Nash said, reluctantly.

Anne carefully took down the information, placed it in a labeled file folder, and stamped *Case Closed* on the outside. Soon it was neatly filed in a cabinet along with other cases.

"Can you get me the telephone numbers of some tree services in the area?" Nash asked.

"Of course, but you know they will all be busy with the cleanup after the storm."

"I know," he agreed, "but there's no way we can move the big stuff. We are gonna need some help."

"And it's going to be very expensive," frugal Anne reminded him.

"I know. And, yes, I know that we do not have the money. I have to trust that it will come from somewhere or the company will let us pay them on the installment plan."

Within a couple of hours, Anne had located a tree service that would come for a reasonable price. They would be there the following day.

"Okay," Anne said. "This is going better than expected. They can be there tomorrow—late morning."

Nash smiled. "Thanks, Anne."

"I'm off to the library. I'll see you Sunday," Anne said, gathering her books together.

The enthusiasm of Friday waned in the face of Saturday's overwhelming task. Louie and Nash were the first to arrive on the scene. The city had promised to remove smaller limbs and debris if they were hauled to the curb. Getting them there would take days, perhaps even weeks.

The two men put on their gloves and started pulling and hauling. The whine of chain saws filled the air. By 9 o'clock, Midge and Clark arrived with some of his football team who had volunteered to help. Katie was next to arrive. By 10:00, everyone was covered with sweat and dirt, but one could hardly see any progress had been made. Ma stopped by with some cool drinks and everyone stopped to refresh themselves and rest. It was difficult to remain positive after so much effort and so little to show for it.

The street had been blocked off except for local traffic so Nash was surprised when he heard vehicles. He strained to identify them. And, then, suddenly he recognized the blue pickup truck and the blonde curls that emerged from its door.

"We heard about the problem," Summer said as she waved to him. "Thought you might like some help."

With that, she put the ramps down on the back of the low boy she pulled and drove her tractor down them. Winter, Spring, and Autumn appeared from the other vehicles, all dressed for work. Nash was overwhelmed.

"I—I can't believe you're here," Nash said as the girls gathered around him.

"What?" Winter said with a twinkle in her incredibly gorgeous eyes. "You think we're all just pretty faces?"

She laughed, and the others joined in.

"Believe me," Nash said, "I would never venture to make such a statement."

Summer took over giving directions to the members of the football team, all of whom were more than eager to please the lovely blonde. Midge and Katie introduced themselves to the other Season sisters as they all worked side by side to clear debris. By noon, everyone was getting tired, particularly those who were not used to working outside. Ma arrived with Mr. Meijer's sandwiches, potato salad, and pickles as well as her own homemade cookies and more cold drinks.

Tony came after working a half day at the garage. Clyde had allowed him to bring the tow truck which was a huge help moving some of the larger pieces of debris.

"I don't know how much more we can ask of the women," Nash whispered to Louie.

"I know," Louie agreed. "They are getting tired. And you know as well as I do that they won't give up. Maybe we should suggest we wait and start again on Monday."

"We can try it."

"Company's coming," Katie said as she pointed down the street.

Nash turned his attention in that direction. At first, he did not recognize the vehicles—several sports cars, a pickup truck, and a silver Dodge Charger. Could it be? Nash was beyond tired, so he was short on patience. He really did not want to deal with Spike and his crew of hoodlums.

Nash's pulse increased as he watched ten of the meanest looking men he had ever seen emerge from the vehicles, and Spike was in the lead heading right for Nash. Nash did not need any more trouble on a day like this from Spike and his gang. Nash realized the gang had probably come to gloat about the disaster the storm had caused.

Nash's dismay, however, did not stop Spike's advance. While Nash was lean and lanky, Spike was built more like a wrestler—compact and heavier through the shoulders. He came right up to Nash and stood so close that Nash could smell the tobacco on Spike's breath. Both Louie and Nash were aware that the rest of the gang had surrounded the two of them.

"Hello, Spike," Nash ventured, trying to put neutrality into his voice.

Spike was slow to speak.

"Heard you had some trouble," Spike finally said with a sneer.

"Some," Nash replied, fighting the impulses that were rising within his body.

Another painful moment of intense silence filled the air during which Nash had bad flashbacks from previous encounters. Finally, Spike cleared his throat and began to speak.

"Me an' the boys here—well, we've come to help."

Nash swallowed hard.

"Help?" he repeated.

"Yeah," Spike said, looking around. "I knew you couldn't handle somethin' like this all by yourself. So, I knew you'd need some *real* muscle."

"As I've told you before, Spike, everybody's welcome at the recreation site. I trust you to lead your men where they are needed most."

"Let's go!" Spike directed his buddies.

Nash stared after them in amazement. Ten fresh bodies made a huge difference. Unknowingly, the Season sisters made a second contribution to the project because their presence caused Spike and his boys to attempt to out-do each other in order to impress them. Nash and Louie just exchanged knowing smiles.

The tree service came and removed the big tree from the remains of the building. They also removed one other tree. When Nash worked out a payment plan with them, the owner even cut his price, claiming it was a worthy project. Nash observed Katie sitting with Summer and Autumn working on a design for the new wooden sign that would be erected—a sign that dedicated the park to Ella Mae Swift. Little by little, those who had been there earlier and needed to leave, left with Nash's thanks. By 5:00 in the afternoon, much had been accomplished, and the women were ready to leave.

All four of the Season sisters approached Nash. Despite the sweaty faces and dirt from the days' work, they were still amazingly attractive. Winter was the first to speak.

"Nash, we just can't thank you enough," she began. "We talked 'til the wee hours of the morning—all of us— including mother and Mr. Wainwright. There's so much we understand now that a few days ago, we didn't know.

"Mr. Wainwright has some ideas to get us back on track financially. He's been so helpful. We own a lot of land and are thinking of dividing it. We have no need for all that property, so he thinks we can sell off some of it for building sites. Of course, we don't want anything too close to our immediate house and yard, so we can still maintain our privacy, but that shouldn't be a problem. And we think Giles may have had the right idea in selling the antiques. That would give us some immediate cash. They are, after all, just physical things. I think we've all figured out what the important things in life are."

Winter looked at her sisters who were smiling and agreeing.

"And mother is an entirely different person now that everything is out in the open—more like the mother we remember. She was trying to shoulder all this by herself. Now it's a group effort, and we're all in it together."

With that, Winter gathered Nash in her arms and hugged him. Each of the girls followed their eldest sister's example, conveying their thanks. Nash's heart was full. He stood for a time watching them as they walked to their vehicles. He hardly realized Louie had joined him.

"Wow!" he said softly. "This personal investigating business sure has its rewards."

"Yep," Nash smiled. "You should try it sometime."

Nash and Louie were ready to call it a day as well. But Spike insisted that his crew work for another couple of hours. At the end of the day, Nash and Louie stood surveying the work. They were both tired but agreed that it had been a good day at Ella's Place.

## 15

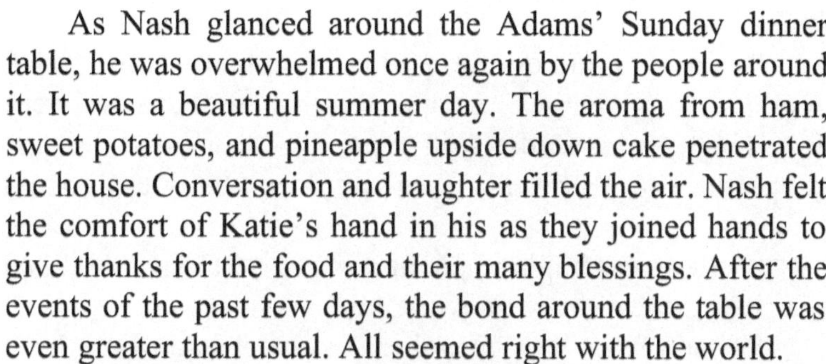

As Nash glanced around the Adams' Sunday dinner table, he was overwhelmed once again by the people around it. It was a beautiful summer day. The aroma from ham, sweet potatoes, and pineapple upside down cake penetrated the house. Conversation and laughter filled the air. Nash felt the comfort of Katie's hand in his as they joined hands to give thanks for the food and their many blessings. After the events of the past few days, the bond around the table was even greater than usual. All seemed right with the world.

"So, I hear you wrapped up the Season case," Tony commented.

"Yes. It all came to an end on Thursday evening."

"There's something I still don't understand," Midge interjected. "Why did Giles take the antiques?"

"Apparently, he overheard a conversation between Holly and Mr. Wainwright—her attorney. It seems that the Season fortune dwindled over time, and Giles assumed he was going to be let go. Since he had been with the Seasons so long and no provision had been made for his retirement, he felt he would end up homeless in his declining years. He planned to sell the antiques to have money to live on if that happened. He believed the family owed him that much."

"Is it true? Are the Seasons broke?"

"Their fortune was in trouble before Stormy passed away. Stormy's inheritance was lost through overspending and mismanagement. He had an addiction to gambling that stemmed back to his college days, so he had gambled away a lot of his family's fortune. I think he panicked when he became ill and realized he was dying. Faulty as his thinking might have been, he wrote the clause into his will in a desperate attempt to keep his family together for as long as possible. He probably thought the girls would be a help to their mother. Instead, it drove a wedge between them. After talking with them yesterday, I'm convinced they will be all right once they work it out together—as a family."

"What's going to happen to Giles?" Anne wanted to know.

"That's a good question," Louie replied. "Holly is not pressing any charges. It appears that she can be very forgiving. As far as the theft goes, the items never left the property. There's not a lot we can do if she doesn't press charges."

"Still, it was kinda stupid of him to give Holly the spiked tea right there in front of everyone."

"That's what happens when a suspect in a crime feels pressured. They start making mistakes. When someone is under that kind of duress, logic goes out the window. It makes my job easier."

"Actually, the same thing could be said of Stormy Season. He felt the stress, or possibly even responsibility for the financial mess. He wasn't thinking logically either."

"I hold Mr. Wainwright responsible, too. He should have directed Holly to sell her excess property immediately under the circumstances, don't you think?"

"That would be my opinion. But who knows?" Nash thought about his conversation with Marjorie Fortune. "We all have a side of us that perhaps others will never know."

"I still don't understand why Giles went to the trouble to get the stuff from Africa when there are plenty of poisons right here in the United States."

"He got the idea right after Winter returned from Africa. We found evidence on his computer that he had researched the subject. With Winter's recent trip to Africa, he thought it was the perfect way to cast suspicion on someone else. If anything ever surfaced, Winter would be blamed, but he thought since she had not done it no one would be able to pin it on her. We also found out that he had talked extensively with Professor Scutter about its use. But Professor Scutter was oblivious to the reason behind the discussions. He just thought Giles was interested in Africa. And, of course, he was more than happy to talk about it."

"When did you know it was Giles?" Midge asked.

"Well, it bothered me when I asked him about the antiques, and he seemed to know each piece in detail. I was going back over the information in my mind and each time the tea kept coming up. I thought it was a lead worth following."

"Did you ever think one of the girls was the culprit?" Katie asked.

"Actually, I did. There were times I was sure it was Summer. For instance, when I found the damaged tire, she was the logical suspect. I think that was Giles' second attempt to cast suspicion on someone else. Everyone knew how handy she was with tools and no one would suspect Giles knew anything about that sort of thing. Other times, the evidence pointed strongly at Winter. I'm kinda glad it turned out to be neither one of them. They are all good people, and they proved it by coming yesterday to help with the cleanup. They were such a blessing. They told me they want to help after we get established. Summer has volunteered to share her knowledge about plants with children from the neighborhood and also will do some landscaping and beautification of the property. And Autumn wants to teach some art classes."

"I'd like to get to know Summer better," Tony interjected wiggling his eyebrows. "A woman who is handy with tools like she is has a certain appeal. And, of course, it doesn't hurt that she's gorgeous."

"Oh, for sure, that needs to be first priority on your list of qualities in a woman, little brother," his sister chastised.

"There's something I don't understand," Katie was puzzled. "I found out she sold that ring. What was that all about?"

"It didn't have anything to do with the case. It turns out it was a gift from one of her suitors. It wasn't even about the money so much as it was the fact that the guy was someone she didn't care to remember."

"I couldn't believe it when Spike and his crew arrived yesterday," Louie added. "We had pretty much thought they were content just to cause trouble. They made a huge difference."

"Just like I always say," Ma spoke up. "There's good in everyone. Sometimes it just takes a little kindness to bring it out."

That was Ma, always finding the good in people, always finding something positive to say about everyone. It was a quality she had passed on to her children.

"I think this entire thing is giving Holly and her daughters a chance to talk and reconnect and move forward. That makes me feel good."

"I'm glad it wasn't any of the girls," Katie said. "I really enjoyed getting to know them and talking with them yesterday. They have good ideas. I think we've worked out a design for the sign. I was impressed."

Just then, Nash's cell phone rang.

"Really? Thank you so much. That's great news. I appreciate all you've done. Good-bye."

All eyes were turned towards Nash asking for an explanation.

"That was Sarah Newcombe from the library. Autumn Season has accepted their invitation to have a showing of her art work next month."

"That's great news," Katie verbalized. "You instigated that, didn't you, Nash?"

"Maybe."

"Of course, you did," Katie continued. "I'll be first in line at the viewing. I've not seen her work, but I thought she was very creative with the sign."

"I'm not a connoisseur of art, but I thought what I saw in the art room was quite good. And I'm also happy that she is getting out of herself. It must be difficult for someone as talented as she is to expose herself to the world of criticism. I'm proud of her for doing this. It will be good for Holly, as well. I think she was so hard on Autumn because Autumn was fulfilling the dream Holly had wanted for herself. Holly pursued art in college but dropped out because she was expecting Winter."

"What is the next step with Ella's Place?"

"For sure, more cleanup. That's going to take some time."

"I've got an idea!" Katie always seemed to sparkle when she had ideas.

"Let's hear it," Midge was interested. "You have such good ideas."

"Why don't we plan a neighborhood picnic—an old-fashioned potluck—whatever you want to call it. Invite the entire neighborhood. We can have it right there on the grounds. People can come and see what we have done and what needs to be done. We need to show everyone that we may have had a temporary setback, but we are coming back with a vengeance. If we plan it a couple of weeks down the road, I know it won't be finished or anything, but it would be something positive, something for people to look forward to. What do you think?"

"I think that's a great idea. Maybe we can get some of the playground usable by then."

"Mr. Pickford has a group that plays music. Maybe they would be willing to share it with us."

"I can check to see if I can get a local television station to show up and give us some air time," Midge offered. "Maybe invite our local councilwoman to attend."

Nash immediately thought of Councilwoman Fortune. He leaned back as he heard the discussion of ideas that bounced back and forth around the table. As the ideas surfaced, so did the spirit of enthusiasm. It was like Mr. Meijer said: No one can take away the spirit of dreaming.

"Who's ready for dessert?" Ma said as she and the girls began to clear the table.

It was unanimous. No one ever turned down any of Ma's desserts.

"Wait!" Tony held up his hand. "I just have one more thing to say."

Everyone stopped what they were doing and looked at Tony.

"What?" Nash frowned.

"I'm just saying," Tony beamed, "if you need my help in any of your future cases, I'm available—for a price."

"What are you talking about?"

"Remember back when you first took the Season case? I believe it was me—your little brother—who solved it that day."

"How do you figure that?"

"Check it out," Tony said proudly. "If you recall, I was the one who said the butler did it. It was me!"

Groans came from around the table as everyone laughed. It was a good day in the Adams' house.

## The End

# Author's Bio

Growing up in the small-town Midwest, G. L. Gracie developed an early interest in literature. Rural schools, country living, a love of horses, and a sturdy moral compass are reflected in her writings. Encouraged by her parents, she often scripted plays for the local church during her tender teenage years. The world of imagination was always at her fingertips, expressed in music and art as well as writing. She loved hearing her grandfather, her parents, and her extended family tell the stories of the "old days" and those have influenced her writing. Short stories and poetry continued to abound during her college years, but her first attempt at writing a novel did not come until 2005. *The White Rose* was finally published in 2014. It was the fourth book to be published and the third in the Rose series.

G. L. Gracie writes mostly for her own enjoyment and rarely knows where her characters will lead her once the story has begun.

"It's a journey I wouldn't miss," she says of her time as an author.

**Books by G. L. Gracie**

*The Rose Trilogy:*
 *Ivy and Wild Roses*
*Sweet Primrose*
*The White Rose*

*Nash Adams Mysteries:*
*Murder Among the Rich*
*Mystery at Chadwick Stables*
*Mystery at Foggy River*
*The Stone Lake Incident*
*Secrets of Lafferty Hill*
*Adele: Case # 625*
*Gray Manor Mystery*
*The Trouble with Seasons*

*Beyond the Dreams:*
*Beyond the River*
*Beyond the Horizon*
*Beyond the Thunder*
*Beyond the Wildflowers*

*Amelia*

*Willow*

*Refuge From the Storm*

*Through the Mist*

*When Magnolias Bloom*

*Countin' Stars*

*Razz A Ma Tazz*

*Whispers of Love*

*Billy*

www.ingramcontent.com/pod-product-compliance
Lightning Source LLC
Chambersburg PA
CBHW030321160726
47992CB00005B/2116